The Pinkest Rose

J.L. Kreutzer

PublishAmerica
Baltimore

First printing

This is a work of fiction set in a background of history. Public personages both living and dead may appear in the story under their right names. Scenes and dialogue involving them with fictitious characters are of course invented. Any other usage of real people's names is coincidental. Any resemblance of the imaginary characters to actual persons, living or dead, is entirely coincidental.

ISBN: 1-4241-0451-3
PUBLISHED BY PUBLISHAMERICA, LLLP
www.publishamerica.com
Baltimore

Printed in the United States of America

Dedicated to
Roy and Eugenia Chord

Acknowledgements

To my husband Bill, for helping me concoct this story, and to my dearest children for listening to me and eating leftovers while I typed.

Special thanks to my friend Abby Watkins, for so generously sharing her time and artistic talent with me.

Chapter 1
Preparing for Company

The storm advanced quickly toward the peak of St. Elmo Mountain, and without warning, lightning flashed threateningly across the night sky. Huge raindrops began to fall from the dark, ominous looking clouds. Jillian Rose Moore felt the emptiness inside of her echo like thunder through the steep canyon walls. Driving through the rain she wondered how her life had become so pointless, so barren in contrast to the pristine beauty of her surroundings.

She noticed that unlike last year, rain had seemed to come more regularly this summer. *At least it will lower the fire danger*, she thought as she tried to stay on the narrow winding road. With its welcome presence a lush, green paradise was growing, carpeting the forest floor of the Black Hills with new pine, spruce and aspen trees. The Black Hills of South Dakota, the hills Jillian had called home all of her life. To her they represented such diversity; a contrast of American presidents and Indian Chiefs, carved into the same granite yet worlds apart in religion and culture. Since the discovery of gold in 1874, folks had been coming steadily to the hills, first as prospectors and eventually as tourists.

Jillian knew better than anyone about the steady streams of tourists who came there like clockwork every year, beginning in early May and ending in late September. They came and visited the shops, restaurants, and galleries, clogging the streets of the little hill towns to see the sights and spend their money. Being a business owner herself, no one understood that tourists are the bread and butter of the local merchants and artists in the area like she did.

From her grandparents, Jillian had inherited a once thriving resort that sat on three and a half acres of prime Black Hills real estate, which was surrounded by towering trees, so rain was always welcome even if it sometimes felt bleak and gray.

Though she was only a forty-something, her stressful life seemed to be draining the youthful vivacity she once felt when the business first became hers so many years ago. Back then she had no idea of the sacrifices she would pay to live out here and operate this business. Letting out a sigh, she thought of the places she had not been able to visit because she was so busy every summer trying to manage the place and make a living.

When she's not frantically working she was alone, and her personal life, what there was of it, had not gone much of anywhere. She was becoming increasingly aware that the years were slipping slowly away from her.

The Lodge, the heart of her business, sat in a winding canyon at the bottom of the northeastern face of St. Elmo Mountain. The 3,000 square foot rustic log cabin, sitting inside a semi-circle formed when the highway was constructed to bow around the toe of the mountain, was where she lived and worked. The aging log structure encompassed two massive rock fireplaces, a kitchen, a large, open dining room and the little apartment Jillian shared with her cat, Tessa. Another attraction to the lodge were the two small fishing ponds and an idyllic little stream that wound its way down the back of the property.

Pulling into the driveway she parks and gazes lovingly at the outer shell of this beautiful log building. It means everything to her. When the burning fireplaces illuminate its many windows the cabin reminds Jillian of a Thomas Kinkade painting, warm and inviting, but tonight there was no fire burning for her, just cold darkness reflecting emptiness through the panes of glass. Though she had closed her grandmother's gift shop last year and made the space into an apartment for herself she felt uneasy that she now lived in the same place where she worked. The idea that there was no separation of the two worlds, no one to take her away from it all or to welcome her home at the end of a long day, filled her with dismay.

Getting out of her car she trudged through a puddle on the path to the front door. Nothing out here could surprise her anymore, as she had seen all manner of weather in her thirty years of living in this canyon, but something about this storm was unnerving her tonight. The air literally crackled with static electricity as the temperature dropped too quickly, instilling the fear that there might be hail in the vicinity. As she fumbled for her keys, she was startled by the lone cry of a coyote howling from somewhere up the Sunday Gulch Trail. Familiar but chilling, it reminded her of her own solitude and resonated with the unrelenting loneliness eating at her soul.

"Home at last," Jillian sighed as she half stumbled through the door. It has been a long day and it felt so good to be home.

Flipping on the lights she threw her jacket carelessly onto the bed and begins to brew a fresh pot of coffee. The anxiety in her chest intensified by the minute as she impatiently awaited the arrival of her family, the Jordans: Uncle Victor, Aunt Carla, their son Jake, his wife, Cindy and their two sons Brian and Greg. Traveling in from California, they were due out there sometime tonight. Jillian absentmindedly pours black steaming coffee into the biggest mug she could find.

Coffee, the nectar of the gods. She smiled as she attempted to figure out where they might be by now in her head.

"Why haven't they called yet?" she said to Tessa, her cat, scratching her lovingly behind her ears and laughed tenderly as Tessa replied with a look of bewilderment. Tessa was a female tabby Jillian found eleven years ago along the road and had kept in high style ever since.

Jillian's California cousins had last visited St. Elmo's Silver Bell Lodge three years ago and though she knew she shouldn't care, their possible reaction to the changes she had made caused her to be anxious anyway.

"How are they going react to me turning the gift shop into this

9

apartment?" she wondered aloud as she straightened up the room.

Wistfully, she remembered how upset her aunt, Carla Jordan, had been after learning that Grandpa Ray had willed this valuable property to Jillian in the first place and she didn't want a repeat of that performance.

Though Carla hadn't said it to her face, Jillian still had the distinct impression her aunt thought she was much too young to handle all of the responsibility. The looks she gave her, the sudden change in her mannerisms made Jillian paranoid, perhaps too much so. Though she had proven her aunt and everyone else wrong, the responsibility had come with a high personal price tag, at least in her mind.

Jillian believed that in his will, Grandpa had tried to make sure each family member was given what he alleged to be a fair piece of the pie. In 1978, the year Grandpa died, his will stated that Carla's family was to inherit the campground across the highway upon the death of the surviving spouse or Carla's mother, as it were. Jillian was aware that Grandma had sold the property in a less than Puritan manner that didn't set well with Aunt Carla and Jillian knew without a doubt that she was still angry about that too.

Jillian's grandparents, Ray and Lugenia Crawford, had purchased the Silver Belle Lodge and another nearby property called the Sleeping Abe Gold Mine in the late sixties with money they had earned mining uranium in the southern Black Hills.

Her Grandfather Ray had taken care of the campground, with the beautiful chalet and the crazy gravity house on the side of the hill. It was his pride and joy. Grandpa had added a swimming pool and a barbeque pit to the campground in 1976, the bicentennial year, and the additions had helped to increase his business.

Even today, Jillian felt injured and empty without the campground still belonging to the family, its beauty being an essential part of her sentimental self. Seeing it there but not being able to step foot on it caused her intense personal pain and she knew Aunt Carla feels the same.

Back in the day, so to speak, Grandmother Lugenia had been in charge of cooking the rainbow trout campers would catch in the pond located on the west end of the lodge nearest to the kitchen. Jillian would watch her grandmother as she encouraged her patrons to purchase Black Hills gold and silver jewelry, trinkets, agates and Indian arrowheads from her gift shop. She had been a shrewd businesswoman, a convincing sales clerk and a really good cook. Seldom did anyone walk out of her establishment without buying something from the gift shop, whether they wanted it or not.

Jillian, admiring Grandma's talents, unknowingly picked up many of her habits and characteristics though she wasn't even aware of it.

Sipping her coffee, Jillian covered her legs with an old afghan and reminisced on how many fond memories this sprawling playground held for her, her brother Ian, and her cousins. She remembered back in 1975, when they hosted an influential political figure and his wife from South Dakota. They had come to spend the weekend in the chalet and caused quite a ruckus amongst the locals and the guests in the campground. The thought of Grandma flitting around with her Queen of Sheba attitude made Jillian smile. Fondly she recalled her grandparents as loving caretakers to her and Ian. She always respected them for stepping in and taking over when their daddy died in the accident up on the Sleeping Abe and life had gotten so difficult for the two of them.

Chapter 2
Expect the Unexpected

Jillian, entranced in poignant thoughts of the past, jumped as her cell phone pierced the quiet evening with a lively ring tone to "The Sting." Momentarily startled by it, she checked the number to see if it was her family on the other end. Relieved that it was finally them, she answered and heard the familiar voice of her beloved Aunt Carla Jordan.

"Jillian, we're at a motel in Rapid City," Aunt Carla yelled loudly into the cell phone, seemingly frustrated at her inability to work it properly. "The weather is absolutely ghastly so we're not coming out tonight, besides it's so hard to see deer with the rain and all."

Jillian chuckled faintly. She knew Carla had only just purchased the cell phone two weeks before the trip and did not trust that the gadget actually works.

"The Good Lord willing, we'll be there for breakfast around 8:00 tomorrow morning, if you don't mind," promised Carla apologetically.

Trying not to sound disappointed, even though logs were burning in the fireplace and cinnamon rolls were wrapped in tin foil warming on the hearth to welcome them, Jillian replied as cheerfully as possible, "Oh that's too bad, Aunt Carla. I was looking forward to seeing all of you tonight, but it's raining cats and dogs out here too. I think it's a good idea to play it safe. I'm really glad you got a room."

"By the way, Jillian," Carla continued, "we brought someone with us."

"Oh really?" Jillian said happily, half expecting it to be her cousin Jennifer. "Who?"

"Do you remember Heath Connors?" Carla blurted out nervously, not sure what to expect from the other end. At once she heard what she thought was a gasp but then again it could just be static from the incessant cell phone, she wasn't sure.

An uneasiness filled the airwaves before either one spoke a word. Permeating the silence with a pensive sigh, Jillian finally replied, "Oh Aunt Carla, please tell me you didn't bring him along."

"Well honey, he thought it was time to come revisit the area." She laughed uneasily. "He was curious if you would offer him a place to stay or if he should get a room in Hill City tomorrow?" Aunt Carla laughed, already knowing her answer.

As a mix of emotions flooded into her mind and tore cruelly at her heart, Jillian attempted to regain some facade of self-control. Desperately trying to gather some cohesive thoughts on the subject, tears began to form in the corners of her eyes as if they had a life completely separate from her ability to control them.

Her brain was not processing the information coming at her from this unexpected announcement. Sitting down hard on the ottoman, Jillian tried to stop her head from reeling with the realization that the only man she has ever allowed to break her heart, to ruin her life completely for that matter, was practically knocking on her doorstep after a twenty–year absence.

"What am I supposed to say?" she whispered as her hand instinctively began rubbing her forehead and temples to relieve her sudden and unexpected headache. She wiped the tears from her cheeks.

"What did you say, honey?" Carla asked loudly, thinking she had lost the phone signal.

"Why sure, bring him on out, we'll dance on the coffee table and have a grand old time." Jillian smirked, just a bit too sarcastically.

"I love you, honey, but if this is too much to ask just let me know," Aunt Carla recanted protectively, sensing she has caused her niece to be seriously upset though not quite sure why.

Trying to protect herself with some distance from this unasked for disturbance in her safe, mediocre life, Jillian replied, "Of course it's not too much to ask, it's…it's just that I don't know if I have enough beds, so he had better not stay here."

Though she knew that what she had just said was a lie, it was the only diversion she could think of on short notice and right now she could care less whether he had a place to stay or not.

I must have forgotten to read the manual that say's this is my problem anyway, she thought angrily.

"Okay honey," Carla replied. "I'll just tell him that he needs to find a motel room. Can't wait to get there, we'll see you tomorrow."

As the conversation ended, Jillian felt a tidal wave of sorrow washing over her, threatening to completely destroy any peace of mind she may have ever concocted for herself. Her mind races to a past that she no longer wanted to acknowledge as she threw the cell phone into the pillow and fell onto the sofa in tears. With her hands over her ashen face, she could feel herself drifting dangerously toward an emotional meltdown.

"Oh my god, how can this be happening? I'm just too busy to have this interruption right now," she shouted as she jumped up and paced wildly around the room.

"How dare he use my family to get back into my life? Who does he think he is anyway; he can't just come back into my life like everything is going to be okay! I mean, how could he have the audacity to just show up after all of these years of not communicating with me, no phone calls or letters, no nothing? God, I don't know if this is a good thing or a bad thing! What's wrong with me?" Jillian wailed loudly.

Terrified at this uncharacteristic display of emotion from her usually docile companion, Tessa ran under the bed for cover.

It was so long ago now, yet feeling as though it was only yesterday, Jillian remembered how Heath had refused to reply to her attempts at communication. She had so much to tell him, yet he had ignored her, rejected her, and brushed her aside like she was a dirty little secret or something.

Their clandestine little affair, buried in a place deep within her, began erupting memories faster than she could repress them. Heaving a log angrily onto the fire, she felt surprise at the ferocity of her resentment after all these years and watched helplessly as sparks flew up the chimney.

Not even her best friend Karen knew what all was going on between them back then; the friend who rarely left her side was completely in the dark about this. Karen didn't know how devastated Jillian felt at Heath's blatant rejection of her because Karen didn't know Jillian had even tried to contact him again. Karen, Aunt Carla and everyone else, thought it was just a casual summer romance because both she and Heath had kept it all very, very private.

Regaining some sense of composure she sat down on the couch and tenderly called Tessa back to her arms. Feeling badly for scaring her cat, her only companion, Jillian decided to take a deep breath to calm down. Watching the soft glow of the embers rekindle into a hot, crackling flame, she couldn't help but feel the irony in it all. Magically, her mind reeled back to 1985, the summer she was 25.

Chapter 3
Mystery Comes Knocking

Allowing herself the luxury of slipping into a past filled with memories of sadness and turmoil, Jillian drifted back to her young adulthood, to her one and only summer of love—1985. She remembered seeing this unusually attractive man who once held her heart in the palm of his hand for the first time. Her memories, though perhaps not quite accurate, were as clear as the day she experienced them.

That particular early July day was perfect, she remembered, with brilliant blue skies and green, dew–kissed grass competing for space below the majestic Ponderosa Pine. The smell of summer in the Hills; the pungent smell of decaying pine needles, or duff, so rich and organic that you just want to hold it to your nose and inhale its earthy fragrance.

It was one of those particularly perfect days when the California clan showed up for their yearly vacation. As soon as their van door opened up in front of the lodge, Heath had leapt out like he owned the place. Jillian immediately took notice of the young man with the curly blond hair that flowed just below his ears. To her amazement nothing covered his long lean torso except a delicious set of chiseled abs. She was startled at the sight of his tanned, rippling muscles, and the audacity he displayed at showing them off.

He definitely wasn't a South Dakota boy, they were much more modest. At least the ones she knew from high school and the few she had actually dated were modest. He had California written all over him, like a flashing neon sign displayed over his head.

Wearing lime green and orange paisley shorts and a pair of Birkenstocks on his long slender feet, her first impression of him was that he had to be a surfer. Adorning his creamy brown eyes were delicate eyelashes that curled slightly on the ends, and Jillian found herself drawn to them like a moth to a flame.

Desperate to find out who he was, Jillian asked her cousin, Jake, to introduce him. Despite her best efforts, Jillian scarcely avoided acting like a giddy schoolgirl as Heath extended his hand toward hers. The attraction was instant and inescapable; they were like magnets hopelessly drawn toward each other.

Within days, this mounting attraction had turned from an innocent flirtation into a fiery love affair. Sneaking up to the Sleeping Abe to spend time alone, they discovered a special place, a lover's nest and a paradise nestled amongst a beautiful outcropping of rose quartz. For three glorious weeks, the old gold mine acted as a passionate point of encounter for the young lovers.

Jillian didn't know any better than to give her heart completely to him because she had never been in love before this. Certainly there had been men in her past, mostly boys, but never someone like him. He knew exactly what he was doing and he took her to places she had never been.

She never suspected he would just leave her, but he vanished from her life as quickly as he had entered it. Though he had promised to keep in touch when he went home to California, her worst nightmares were confirmed when he returned the letters she had sent to the address Jake had given her.

In August, she realized that she was pregnant. Panic-stricken, she cried out, "Oh God, what do I do now?"

Fully aware of his memory growing inside of her, the reality of the situation slowly sank in as Jillian tried to make plans for her future as a single mother.

The issue of how to run the restaurant and take care of a baby at the same time became overwhelming. Though she loved children, she knew this was going to be the most difficult challenge life had ever thrown at her. Raising a baby without Heath, running a restaurant at her young age and keeping her sanity was going to be the trial of the decade.

Just as acceptance began to permeate her mind, Jillian found her body unexpectedly purging the pregnancy and she lost the baby in her twelfth week. Not only had she lost the man she loved passionately but his child was ripped from her, body and soul as well. She told no one.

As time went by, she realized this had been the only opportunity God had given her to experience the joy of pregnancy. She had spent the time being miserable, thinking only of herself. For the sake of the child, she knew in her soul that she should have taken it easier and not worked so hard. She wondered if she unconsciously did it on purpose.

As her daydream morphed into a guilt-ridden nightmare, the painful memories of it all seized her stomach into a tight ball. Trembling, she stares at the now cold ashes in the fireplace, feeling as empty and dirty as the cavern in front of her.

"How can I ever face Heath Connor again? I hate him," she asked her kitty quietly.

The darkness of the room imitated the black hole that she knew had resided in her soul for much too long.

"Why, after so long, is God making me face this again?"

Bitter tears slid slowly down the sides of her cheeks. Sorrow, not cutting her as intensely as it once had, came over her with a stinging, steady realization that she had lost her golden opportunity to be a mother. Though she had asked God for forgiveness she struggled to forgive herself.

Even though she had tried her whole life to always do the right thing, she felt God continually punished her by systematically taking the people she loved the most out of her life, leaving her alone. As exhaustion took its toll, Jillian finally fell into a fitful, uneasy sleep.

Chapter 4
Life as Usual

As her eyes adjusted to the light she realized that it was already 6:15 a.m. The sky, showing no sign of the prior evening's fury, began to softly paint the granite spires a faint golden hue. Birds were chirping outside her window so loudly that they finally woke her up.

"Oh no, what time is it? I hate waking up late!" she growled as she stumbled stiffly towards the bathroom.

In the mayhem of the night she had forgotten to set an alarm clock. Pouring herself into the shower she could feel the warm soapy water washing away some of the poignant memories of the prior evening and she felt so much better.

Pulling her dark brown, shoulder-length hair up into a bun, she sloughed on some make-up. Quickly dressing, Jillian noticed she seldom wore anything but simple clothing anymore, usually just jeans, a tee shirt and tennis shoes to support the feet she was on all day. She wrapped a clean apron around her waist and surveyed herself in the mirror.

"God, everything I own looks the same—plain!" she sighed, looking drearily at her outfit.

As she stared at her reflection her self doubt was amplified as the reality of the day ahead sunk in, quickly making her angry all over again.

"I don't care anyway! I'm not dressing up for His Majesty's

arrival," she stated stubbornly, trying to convince herself that what he thought doesn't matter.

I'm not playing games with him anymore, she thought. *I don't feel like getting hurt this late in my life. I just won't allow it.* With a determined turn, she walked toward the kitchen and dismissed all remaining thoughts of Heath from her mind.

Turning her attention back to the restaurant, she realized that because she had overslept, everything was now running thirty minutes behind. She has been her own boss most of her life, ever since taking over the restaurant at age 20, but today she didn't feel as in control or as responsible as she usually expected herself to be.

Since she was a child, Jillian had known what it took to run the lodge. The premise of her operation was simple—she charged her customers a modest price per inch for the rainbow trout that they caught in the pond. Then she gutted, filleted, breaded and fried their catch on the big grill in the kitchen and served it in the dining room along with a salad, rice pilaf, fresh baked bread and a drink.

Most people didn't realize what a bargain her prices actually were, but she was very aware of the success her grandmother had with the pond before she inherited it and decided to continue the tradition.

Planning to do all of the labor herself—cooking, cleaning the fish, and waiting on customers—soon became an overwhelming task. Jillian found herself amazed at the unanticipated affection the locals had towards her cooking, though deep down she knew she was good at it and her restaurant had an ambiance that was unrivaled in her area.

Finally accepting the fact that she was going to need a little help, she began gathering a modest group of applicants that she felt would best serve her customers with the type of kindness and compassion that she, herself, had given them.

In the end, Jillian made the decision to hire her best friend Karen Sanderson and Roxie Hall, a young single mother from Texas trying with all of her might to keep her head afloat, to help her cook and wait tables.

They both came in at 10:00 a.m. religiously during the week and worked the weekends as well. She couldn't appreciate them more if she tried. They were a godsend to her, as their presence took much of the burden off of her shoulders, and freed her to deal with public relations, which had always been her favorite part of running the lodge anyway.

Even with the additional employees, what she needed most was someone to take over the operation of the fishing shack. Though she had advertised in the local newspaper, no one had applied. Jillian realized it was a pretty crummy job, all things considered: digging night crawlers, skewering them onto a hook, making small talk with the customer while they waited for the big moment when a fish took their bait. The job was very time consuming and her time had become very valuable, so she continued to advertise, hoping someone would respond.

Jillian's workweek rotated around delivery trucks that brought the supplies necessary for the restaurant. When they arrived, they demanded her full attention. She always dropped whatever task she was currently working on to sign their invoices and check in merchandise. The drivers were her connection to the outside world, and she had made it a point to know all of their names, how many kids they had, and what they were up to.

Besides the delivery trucks, the lawn service came and mowed every Wednesday morning. The large grassy knoll in front of her restaurant was full of sweet-smelling purple clover. As a child, Jillian spent hours looking for four-leaf clovers, but her carefree days were gone, and she missed them all dearly. Now she was an adult, a workhorse, and she longed for those carefree days again when responsibility wasn't even something she considered.

Swinging the big, wooden doors to her kitchen open, she loudly announces her presence to absolutely no one but the four walls and to the furniture that no one sat in.

"Good morning," she sighed as the emptiness of her life once again set in harshly.

It's not that she longed to be alone. It simply had worked out that way. But at least she had Tessa. Filling Tessa's dish with dry cat food and fresh water, her thoughts drifted towards her grandmother, who had added this kitchen in 1972 as an addition to the original structure of the lodge, and to Jillian's father, Avery Moore, who had helped build it with his own two hands. Jillian felt a deep connection to the past each time she entered the kitchen.

Looking around, the kitchen literally echoed with emptiness, but by turning on the grill, the deep fat fryers and the two ovens used for her daily baking chores, everything began to change, even if only by appearance. The room began to radiate heat and sound, light and smell, just as if it were a living, breathing entity. Certain smells made the past spring to life and serve as a reminder to Jillian of a happier day when her whole family would gather here to eat. This simple thought brought her daily joy.

Chapter 5
A Change in the Wind

Right on cue, Jillian watched out the window as the three vehicles pulled up the long horseshoe shaped driveway and parked next to the kitchen. Taking a deep breath to calm her nervousness, she tentatively stepped out onto the deck to face the firing squad.

"Jillian, give me a hug. We've missed you!" Aunt Carla exclaimed excitedly as she came bounding toward her with her arms outstretched.

"I've missed you too, Aunt Carla!" Jillian cried out joyfully.

As she took turns hugging each family member, a feeling of relief that their journey had played out without any mishaps flood over her. In Jillian's mind they all drove too fast and she constantly worried when they were on the road.

"Wow, that van is pretty wild for an old codger like you, Jake," she teased her cousin as he exited his vehicle.

Jake was driving a perfectly restored 1968 Volkswagen Microbus that sported a Ken Keesey bumper sticker that says, *"Can You Pass the Test?"* The van was already attracting a couple of fifty-year-old men from the campground who were eagerly making their way over to the lodge to admire it.

Letting his arm rest casually around her shoulder, Jake smiled devilishly at her witty comment. Giving her a quick peck on the cheek he asked, "You like it?"

It was important to him that she liked it. What she thought had always been important to him because she was sensible and he knew she would tell him if she thought he was acting immature.

"Very cool, very California, Jake," she exclaimed. "I especially like the bumper sticker and the Grateful Dead dancing bear in the back window. I love it! When can we go for a ride?"

Jillian and Jake had always been close friends. They had a lot in common: they were the same age, loved going to the same social events when they were younger, like rock concerts and all night beer parties, yet both had the good sense to stop their wild ways a good twenty years ago.

Though she tried not to notice it, tried to pretend it didn't exist, her eyes couldn't help but wander over to the black SUV parked beside Jake's van. Her thoughts had become nearly obsessive with the question of how she was going to react to seeing Heath again. She couldn't help but remember their first encounter and how she had acted like a love sick puppy, but she was absolutely determined not to repeat that performance again.

As near as she could tell the SUV was expensive, a Cadillac Escalade perhaps, hiding its occupant covertly behind dark windows, shielding his identity as if to add drama to his grand entrance back into her life.

At this point Jillian was trying to act cool and collected, but knowing she was being watched behind the dark shading gave him an unfair advantage over her and it made her angry all over again.

Jake, feeling Jillian's anxiety, subversively leads her toward the SUV while innocently immersing her in conversation as a distraction. "So, what's the latest news from Rapid City?"

"Not much, Jake, it started to rain again so there haven't been any fires yet this year, that's always a relief, sitting out here in the forest like this," she replied still looking at the Escalade, squinting her nose trying to see inside. "What's he doing, taking a bath in there?"

"Not sure, dear! Who's playing at the Civic Center this summer? I heard Crosby, Stills and Nash were here a while back. Man, I would have loved to have seen that." He didn't miss a beat.

"I went to it, wouldn't have missed it for anything. Only wish you were here to go along with me is all," Jillian said as she noticed the door opening.

Suddenly, Heath was facing her, looking as handsome and healthy as he had twenty years before, not looking at all like the boogie man she had conjured up in her mind.

"Dang," she said under her breath, hoping Jake missed it.

With her heart racing and adrenaline pumping, she once again found herself examining his handsome features. His eyes were still as she remembered them, though lines had formed softly around the edges, but they were still as breathtaking and beautifully brown as they had been when she first lost herself in them, and though gray hair surrounded the temples, his hair was still so touchable, with wisps of blond interlaced throughout his gorgeous head.

Heath came bounding toward her, shaking her back to reality.

"Nice to see you again, Cookie, it's been a long time," he exclaimed with a fervor that startled her to her toes. She couldn't believe he remembered that after all these years.

Embracing her like she was his long lost best friend, he twirled her in a circle.

Pushing away, she replied cautiously to him, "Nice to see you too, Heath."

"Bet you never thought you'd see me again?" Heath mused playfully.

"Haven't really thought much about it actually, now that you mention it," Jillian jabbed sarcastically, wondering how she came up with that lie on the spur of the moment.

Not wanting to give him the impression that she was in the least bit interested, she politely straightened her apron and turned toward the kitchen. As a means of escaping this awkward situation, Jillian did what came naturally to her, she offered to cook.

"Come in everyone, I'm sure your starving, let me fix you something to eat," she exclaimed tensely, all the while ready to bolt like lightning if he even breathed wrong. She was aware everyone was watching her reaction to seeing him again.

She could feel her emotions coming to a broil inside her head. Once nervous and uncertain, they were now turning to irritation and impatience as she realized that he still had an effect on her.

It's a conspiracy, plain and simple, and they're all in on it together, she rationalized.

Heath called out to her as he walked back toward his vehicle, "Wait a minute, Jillian, I want you to meet my two hooligans here in the back seat sleeping. Hey, Kaitlyn, Ryan, wake up, we're here. I have someone here I'd like you to meet."

Jillian turned awkwardly towards them as her jaw nearly dropped to the ground in disbelief. She could have been knocked over with a feather at this point. No one had mentioned to her that Heath had children.

No one bothered to mention that he was even coming, so why should I be surprised by this? Jillian thought bitterly, realizing she was dangerously close to tears again. Knowing she didn't want to go there she swallowed the lump in her throat and puts on her best big girl face even as her heart was breaking.

He actually has children, she thought, knowing they could have been theirs if he wouldn't have just used her up and spit her out.

Kaitlyn and Ryan stumbled sleepily out of the back seat of the truck and shook Jillian's hand politely as their father introduced them one at a time.

"Jillian, these are my kids. My pride and joy! Ryan is seventeen and Kaitlyn, my baby girl, is almost fourteen. They're growing up so fast."

She could tell that he was proud to be sharing them with her, though she didn't fully comprehend why he has brought them all this way without their mother.

Straightening her shoulders, she greeted them warmly while trying to hide her profound shock from the children.

"Nice to meet you, Ryan and Kaitlyn, glad you could come."

Rubbing their eyes, they began to come to the realization they had finally reached their destination—the Black Hills.

"Wow dad, look at this place, it's really cool," remarked Ryan.

At seventeen the young man towered over his dad by a good three inches. He looked like a young pup trying to grow into his enormous feet, but Jillian could tell he was on his way to becoming a very handsome young man. *Just like his father*, she thought.

"This is the place I have been telling you about son; I had the best time of my life here one summer," Heath remarked, supposedly to Ryan yet looking at Jillian.

I didn't realize I was just a good time, Jillian smiles with a forced façade that makes her face feel like she was part wicked witch and part actress. Knowing his innuendo was probably not aimed just at her, Jillian still took it personally. Turning away from him, trying to disguise the hurt that was sitting right on her shoulder; she hastily walked into the kitchen. Following her lead, the crowd made their way into the kitchen behind her.

Finding it hard to focus, Jillian noticed that in their excitement everyone was talking at once: her Uncle Victor, describing his rodeo cowboy wounds that seem to endlessly be bothering him, and her Aunt Carla, surprisingly going off about some money issues she was worried about. The four teenagers wasted no time getting to know the place and took off toward the fish pond.

Focusing on Jake, Jillian listened politely as he begins to tell her about his job with a computer company in the Valley. She noticed that he was concentrating on looking first at her and then at Heath, as if willing the two of them to connect, to make eye contact with each other. She recognized that he was most likely the sneaky little matchmaker who set this whole plan into action.

With only her lips moving, Jillian motioned to Jake, "I know you had something to do with this," and shoots him a pointed look across the table.

Jake smiled at Jillian from behind Heath's head after picking up her obvious innuendo. Aunt Carla shook her head and puts her hand over her eyes, as she too became aware of their juvenile behavior behind Heath's back. Heath was sitting in his chair, oblivious to the cousin's unspoken facial language. He was lost in his own thoughts and had his own agenda. He was as close to Jillian's path as he could be, trying not to be too obvious that he was making every attempt to touch her, just to brush up against her hand, her knee, or whatever it took to feel her skin next to his.

"Hey Jake, it really was nice of Jillian to let us come visit, don't you think? After all, there are quite a few of us here," Heath offered kindly, trying to break the ice.

Jake nodded and mumbled agreeably, "Yeah, thanks for having us, Jillian," but then turned away from the table, walked over to the sink as if to put his coffee cup in it and winked at her while no one was watching.

At that moment Jillian knew, like she had never known anything else, that Jake set this meeting into motion and that she was going to kill him for it. From behind the plate rack that sat over the grill, she scowls the best scowl she could at him, baring teeth and all.

Jake saw her and laughed, but says nothing.

Heath turns toward Jillian just in time to notice her less than jovial facial expression toward Jake and wondered what is going on. Figuring it had to do with him, he pretended not to notice and feel no animosity toward either of them. In fact, he was actually enjoying the pantomime going on around him and figured Jillian was letting Jake know in her own little way that she was probably not too happy about his tagging along. He decided to just sit quietly and let her get used to his presence.

Immersing himself with past thoughts, Heath finished his first cup of coffee. Remembering how he had been engaged when he first met Jillian, he always wished that he would have told her, but he doubted she would care to hear any of his lame explanations now! Yet, his mission was clear in his mind. He desperately wants to convince her that he was then and is still in love with her. Her memory burned brightly in him, fueling his desire to get to know who she was now as opposed to who she used to be, feeling sure that her personality was just as attractive as it ever was, though she wasn't really showing it so far.

Continuing to follow her with his eyes, trying to win her over, he could feel the strings of his heart pulling longingly toward her. Wanting to just reach out and touch her, he patiently waited for her to acknowledge him. He couldn't help but notice the way her hair fell delicately across her eyes and the way her smile curved up slightly when she didn't think he was looking.

He realized that some might not see the beauty behind the mask of plain clothes that she was wearing, but to him the simple things about her only added to her charisma and sparked hot thoughts of desire in him. He found her beautiful in her simplicity. Up to this point in time he knew he had done everything wrong and his chances of changing her mind about him were slim to none.

I would hate me too if I was in her shoes, he thought, admonishing himself for his past actions.

As the conversations continued, Jillian served her family breakfast and founds herself compulsively refilling Heath's coffee cup. Instead of calming down in his presence, a nervous perspiration broke out under the back of her collar and she began to feel ruffled and imposed upon.

He keeps staring at me, she thought fretfully. *God I wish he would stop doing that!*

"So Jillian, where would you suggest we stay in Hill City?" he said too abruptly and too loudly and startled her so completely she almost poured hot coffee into his lap.

Practically jumping out of her skin, she realized his incessant staring had now turned to an attempt at conversation. She felt so shaken that she didn't know how to reply.

Wanting to say something mean, she found herself unable to concentrate on words as her eyes meet his, only for a moment, but in that brief instant a blaze of emotion passed between them and they both recognized it for what it is. Shaking off an unwanted notion of desire, she tried to regain her composure by remembering her wounded pride with renewed fervor. Not knowing if he was still married but suspecting he was, she could feel his betrayal stabbing into her heart as though it were a dagger.

How dare you show up here after what you've done to me? she thought as fury throbbed painfully through her head once again. *Your phony California tan and those lying eyes aren't fooling anyone,*

29

least of all me, she reasoned resentfully as heat came up her neck and moved stealthily into her cheeks.

"How about you stay in a cardboard box out back?" she lashed out at him. Knowing this comment was nasty and rude, she could not for the life of her stop herself from saying it.

Heath glared at her, totally speechless. He was a Gemini, and though they are well known for their ability to talk, not a single word was coming to his disposal right now. Suspecting something like this was lurking just under the surface, he figured he just better sit there and take it. He knew he deserved her wrath and was ready, willing and able to deal with it.

There is probably a lot more where that came from, he thought, *and I can't wait to clear the air between us and start over.*

With uneasiness hanging heavily in the air, Aunt Carla jumped up and began to clear the table as a quick diversion to save her niece any more embarrassment, chattering all the while.

"Jillian, let me help get these dishes done," she said cheerily. "Do you have any rubber gloves? I just got my nails done and you know me, I wouldn't want to break a nail doing dishes."

"Yes I do as a matter of fact," Jillian replied, thankful for the distraction but unable to apologize. "They're under the sink in that little blue caddy. Let me help you."

The men took this as an opportunity to flee the kitchen and rapidly made their way to the front porch to finish their coffee and fuss over the little bus that had somehow emerged from the sixties unscathed.

"I don't think that went so well," Heath said to Jake, shaking his head back and forth.

"Me neither," Jake replied as he patted his long time friend knowingly on the back. "Me neither.

Chapter 6
All Mad Things must Come to an End

With the breakfast food put away, the dishes done and the lunch special in the oven, Jillian quickly helped her family unload their luggage into her apartment. Apparent by their expressions, she could feel their approval toward the changes she had made and it brought her some measure of relief. Carla knew Jillian wasn't making enough money on the gift shop to justify the time it took to maintain it. She was happy Jillian had decided to move into the lodge instead of living in the decaying old house across the road and told her so.

"Aunt Carla, you and Cindy make yourselves at home," she ordered, lifting her arms in a grand gesture as though she is one of Bob Barker's beauties showing off the latest merchandise to be won. "Be it ever so humble, there's no place like home."

"It's perfect, Jillian, so homey. I love this country cabin motif you've used to decorate with. It's just adorable," Cindy replied.

"Thanks, I like it too. I've always liked bears. I know there aren't any bears roaming around in the wild around here but they're just so darned cute I couldn't help but mix them in with the bison and the fish. Makes me feel like a natural woman," she half sang to her favorite Carol King lyric.

31

Jillian had suspended a small canoe from the ceiling and filled it with cascading plants that were growing in every direction and wrapping themselves elegantly around the enormous open log rafters.

"You are so clever, girl, who would have thought to do that?" Cindy remarked.

"Oh yeah, it looks good, but once a week I have to drag a ladder in here to water them. As if I don't have enough to do around here I create unnecessary chores for myself." She chuckled.

"It's still unique and the enjoyment you must get from looking at it would make the watering time well worth it to me, Jillian," Cindy replied.

"That's why I keep it up there, its fun to look at. Now, if you'll excuse me ladies, I have fish to feed. Unpack, help yourself to anything you need and I'll see you back here in a little bit."

Certain that her family was comfortable, she took off toward the pond to feed the fish their first meal of the day.

She felt excitement when the four kids, Brian, Greg, Kaitlyn and Ryan, trailed noisily behind her towards the pond. As they became busy throwing in pellets of food they asked a barrage of questions about catching, cleaning and filleting fish. Jillian pledged to show them how it was done and assured them it would be a grand idea if they wanted to try their hand at it later in the day.

"I've been fishing a hundred times," Ryan announces. "I could help you while we are here if you want me too."

Jillian felt pleasantly surprised at his offer and realized that Heath has done a good job teaching his children manners and poise around adults.

"Yeah, that would be great, I would love that."

Not to be outdone, Brian, two years younger than Ryan, piped in, "Me too, I can help too, I don't know how to clean fish but I can feed them and stuff."

Nodding yes, she exclaimed, "This is too good to be true! Two helpers, how wonderful!"

She felt comfortable with them and she laughed spontaneously as she watched them enjoying the pond. The very fact that these city kids were becoming acquainted with a natural environment—the frogs, the cattails, the numerous insects, the fish—was enough to make her feel like a biologist and she laughed at the thought.

Out of the corner of her eye she caught sight of Heath, hands in his pockets, slowly sauntering in her direction.

Oh great, just what I need, she thought. Rolling her eyes, she tried to shake off a totally perturbed feeling at his presence.

Just stay aloof, act uninterested and he'll go away, she thought, though suspecting the reason for her upset was that somewhere, in a place to frightening for her to face, she did not really want him to go away just yet, because curiosity had begun to get the best of her.

Where is his wife, she wondered, *and why didn't he bring her along?*

On the other hand, if there was no wife, he still had treated her badly in the past and she knew she was not going to give him the opportunity to repeat his past performance. She didn't feel like being in a rebound relationship from some messy divorce or his second choice because his Barbie doll–looking California girl took off with someone else.

Heath, looking elegantly casual in his customary Birkenstock sandals, a pair of knee length Bill's khaki shorts and a white tight, sleeveless, wife beater tee-shirt, walked over to the big cardboard barrel she kept the fish pellets in. He uncovered the metal lid used to deter raccoons and deer, scooped out a handful of food and nonchalantly threw a few of the pellets out into the pond. He laughed unexpectedly as twenty fish attacked the food all at the same time.

"Hi Daddy!" Kaitlyn waved affectionately from the far side of the pond. He waved back lovingly at his daughter and then turned to Jillian.

"How many blasted fish you got in this pond anyway, Cookie?" he asked, smiling easily at her, pretending he had not heard her earlier comment about sleeping in a cardboard box.

"Just about enough," she replied and immediately regretted the curtness of her own voice. "I'm sorry, Heath, I didn't mean that," Jillian said in a low voice so the children would not over hear. "It's just that you are about the last person I expected to see. Forgive me for asking, but what are you doing here anyway?"

Heath, realizing he was upsetting her again, tried to remain calm despite the obvious edginess in her voice.

"I'm thinking of moving to the Black Hills with my kids," he replied cautiously, yet for the past month he has rehearsed this line over and over in his mind, wondering what her reaction to it was going to be.

Heath leaned in toward Jillian. Feeling his intensity bearing down on her, she instinctively took a step away from him and sucked in the air that has escaped from her lungs. She noticed for a brief moment his masculinity and a maturity in his demeanor that had not been there before.

"What?" Jillian stammered, not believing her ears. "What do you want to do that for?"

"I'm looking for a new beginning for us. The kids and I have had a pretty rough time lately and I think a change in scenery would be good for all of us," he replied with a sadness that melted the tough exterior she was trying to put on in front of him.

He's had a rough time, she thinks, *he should walk a day in my shoes and then he'll really understand what a rough time is.*

But unexpectedly, from somewhere in the far reaches of her heart, she felt empathy, not just for him but for all three of them. She wondered what had happened, but realized this was neither the time nor the place to be asking.

"Jillian, I have a lot that I would like to talk to you about. Would you have dinner with me tonight? We could have a nice, quiet meal that someone else cooks for a change. What do you say? Will you at least think about it?"

He's been here for 48 minutes and already had the nerve to ask me out! That must be some kind of a record, she thought smugly, turning slightly away from him to think this question through, already knowing what the answer is.

She felt the noose of twenty years of resentment and anger at him losing its grip on her, and realizing she was actually feeling excited about the proposition of a date, she thought, *What the heck, it's not like I have anything better going on and this could be very interesting.*

"Heath, I don't think I'm ready for the nice, quiet meal thing just yet, but I would be willing to go to Flintstone Village and walk around with a bag of popcorn or something like that. Besides, the little train is kind of fun to ride on and we would be on neutral ground."

Chuckling seductively at her nervousness, he asked, "Do we need neutral ground, Cookie, after what we have shared?"

Jillian gave him the look, the look that said emphatically, "Take it or leave it."

Realizing she wasn't kidding he replied without hesitation, "Okay, it's a deal, I would love to visit Fred and Wilma's place this evening."

Laughing out loud, partly because he consented to her idea and partly because she detected a tone of exasperation in his voice, Jillian felt for the first time this entire morning that the ball just might be in her court.

Surprised that this went better than he had anticipated, Heath, grinning gleefully, said, "I'll pick you up at six then."

"Great, I'll be ready."

He grabbed her hand and gave it a little squeeze. "I've got to make some sleeping arrangements in town so were going to take off."

"Okay."

"See you later?" he said, feeling giddy with excitement.

"I'll be ready."

She watched with a heavy heart as Heath and his nice little family pulled down the drive, out onto the highway, and faded into infinity.

Chapter 7
Remembering the Past

Jillian found herself staring blankly into the muddy waters of the pond. Rushing quickly through her mind, a past filled with emotion took her on a trip down memory lane to 1972.

Jillian heard the faint sound of Uncle John's Band playing from the eight-track Ian and Grandpa Crawford had just installed in the used pick-up they bought the weekend before from an auction in Rapid City. The pick-up was an industrial looking 1959 Omaha orange International, retired from the South Dakota D.O.T., but you would have thought it just rolled off the delivery rack from Detroit.

Ian was fourteen that summer, itching to drive like all boys his age, so Grandpa took him into town and bought him a sturdy, low geared four-wheel drive truck, one with lots of metal around him so he wouldn't be as likely to kill himself in it. Ian was so proud and excited to learn how to drive that he couldn't stay out of it.

The small step-side box with the split-up wooden deck, and the chains that held the tailgate, clanking back and forth with every motion, brought pure satisfaction to her brother's face.

In the top right corner of the windshield the rubber seal had shrunk away from too much sun, leaving a gap that sifted mica–impregnated dust into the cab. An old quilt from bygone days covered the springs sticking up from worn out upholstery under the driver's seat; the seat where Ian sat struggling to let out the clutch without killing the engine.

Traveling up and down the road to the Sleeping Abe all that summer; up over the exposed roots of the pine trees, around the granite rocks sticking randomly out of the hillside, made Ian very adept at controlling this bucking bucket of bolts.

Ray Crawford didn't have to do what he did for Ian. He wasn't even his real grandfather, but you would never know it because he treated them both like he was. In fact, Jillian wondered if he had forgotten that little detail.

He was actually Grandmother's second husband. He had been in their lives since she was born though, and she loved him regardless of that fact. The life he had lived seemed so interesting; with enough grand ideas to inspire even the faint of heart, and his enthusiasm for living was contagious.

Sitting at his knee as a child, Jillian would listen to the stories he would tell of his rough and tumble days as a miner.

She had heard that his parents were of Irish Catholic decent and that he had numerous brother and sisters in the East. Instead of staying behind and selling goods in the family mercantile, he had bucked tradition and had come out west to homestead. The terrible drought of the 1930s had caused Ray to call it quits and find work in Sturgis. Though he had to sell his land and cattle he never looked back, only forward to the future.

During those dry, dust bowl days, Ray kept himself abreast of the many exciting changes going on in the Black Hills. He knew Gutzon Borglum was up there working on that mountain, Mount Rushmore they called it, since October of 1927. In 1937, he recalled hearing that two hundred and sixty-five thousand people had come to see what that crabby old sculptor had accomplished. He kept his ear to the ground and in 1939, the last dedication held to mark the fiftieth anniversary of South Dakota's statehood, Ray knew that Mt. Rushmore had become a bonafide tourist attraction and he wanted a piece of the action.

Always an entrepreneur, he hoped to capitalize on the tourist trade by purchasing a dilapidated old grocery store just north of Sturgis. As a gifted handy man, he turned the broken down building into a little business that barely, but effectively, eked out a living for him.

He was doing okay for himself as far as that goes, but the day Lugenia Moore walked into his grocery store, he suspected that his simple life was about to change directions forever.

She was beautiful and destitute, and looked to be just the kind of woman who needed a man. Not any man, mind you, but him specifically. She was a single mother looking for a job to help support her son Avery and her little black-haired daughter with the creamy white skin.

"That little girl looks just like that Disney guy's rendition of Snow White, but cuter," he told her momma as he handed her a penny candy. "What's her name?"

"Her name is Carla," Lugenia replied. "And what's your name, handsome?"

Jillian heard that story every year of their anniversary. She adored it. Ray fell in love with the whole family quickly and married her grandmother within the year.

Jillian tried to imagine what the life of a single mother may have been like in the late '30s. She couldn't imagine that women like her grandmother were very popular in society, but circumstances were such that Lugenia couldn't help it; her husband had run off on her and hadn't come back.

Her grandmother had been abandoned by a man named Martin Eugene Moore. Jillian had always felt angry at him even though she did not know what had ever become of him. As far as anyone knew, Grandma Lugenia had never heard from him again, leaving her with two young children to fend for herself. Why hadn't he tried to contact his family? Did he die on his journey home? She never knew.

She was aware that this man, her real grandfather, had once been a schoolteacher in Missouri. Though she didn't know what he had taught, she knew he had given it all up to come to the Sturgis area for the same reason everyone did—land.

Grandma Lugenia's parents had a farmstead close to his. When Martin Moore came courting for a wife, her parents happily agreed to an arrangement for marriage as they were poor and needed one less mouth to feed. After Martin and Lugenia married it seemed that one calamity after another befell them and they lost everything to a prairie fire when drought overtook the Midwest in the 1930s.

About the same time Ray Crawford gave up homesteading, Martin Moore gave it up too and went back to Missouri looking for work, never delivering on his promise to send for his family. Jillian felt a kinship to her grandma, knowing they had both had similar problems with men. Abandonment just seemed like the gift that kept on giving in this family.

In Jillian's mind, Ray Crawford came to the rescue on more than one occasion. His real love, besides Jillian's grandma, was geology and mining. By the beginning of World War II they had spent several uneventful years running the store and out of sheer boredom, Lugenia finally convinced Ray they needed to pursue their dream of mining.

Gold mining had pretty much played itself out in the hills by the 1940s, but uranium was soon to take its place. Ray knew uranium was being sought after from the government, and miners in the Southwest were making plenty of money from it, so pulling an old trailer house behind a worn out International pick-up truck, his favorite brand, the Crawfords set off to learn the art of locating and mining uranium.

Ray had contacts in the Southwest desert who taught them what types of geological formations uranium could be found in. On their way home from Utah, they passed through the modest, little railroad and cattle town of Edgemont, located in the southwestern corner of the southern hills.

North of town, the muddy Cheyenne River meanders sleepily toward what is now Angostura Reservoir, and just north of the river beautiful, rugged sandstone canyons with names like Red Canyon, Craven Canyon, Hell's Canyon and Teepee Canyon, were once home to Native American Sioux Indians.

The Crawfords, discovering that the rock formations in that area were loaded with "that beautiful ore," as Lugenia referred to it, packed up their two young children, their few worldly possessions, and headed off to their new life as prospectors in Edgemont. They bought a discounted scintillator, used to detect radiation, and staked hundreds of claims, registering them at the land office in Hot Springs, the county seat of Fall River County.

Claim jumpers gave them a hard time in the beginning. Once Lugenia stood in front of a bulldozer to save their mining claims from the "rabble rousers," her favorite term for the men intent on stealing from them, while Ray was getting a lawyer trying to stop the men and their machinery from illegally trespassing on their property. Yet after a rocky beginning and plenty of lawyers' fees, they went on to spend the next 25 years doing what they both loved best—mining uranium.

Jillian knew that they had become very wealthy from their mining endeavors because Ray and Lugenia had sold their interest in the company just as uranium was becoming a dire word in environmental circles. With some of their money they had purchased St. Elmo's Silver Bell Lodge, essentially returning to the retail-type business. At the same time, they also purchased the nineteen-acre claim called the Sleeping Abe gold mine, and an additional 250 acres of untouched, undamaged real estate on the eastern slope of St. Elmo.

Jillian turned her gaze from the pond toward St. Elmo Mountain. She knew it to be a tree-covered peak, majestic and rugged, with gold running deep through its veins. Back in the late 1800s, its pristine beauty was forever altered from the effects of mining. Shafts, or deep tunnels, were dug into its belly, giving no thought to the long-term environmental damage being caused, and Jillian knew sadly that this magnificent mountain still bore the scars of gold fever to this day.

The Sleeping Abe was once a hard rock gold mine, located on the eastern slope of St. Elmo. Grandpa had told Jillian that during its hey day, the Sleeping Abe had been a working gold mine with a large mill situated over the deep tunnels to process the mined ore, but she knew that now the mill was just dilapidated and dangerous.

Grandpa had said that the mill was originally built on the Sleeping Abe to process the ore taken from St. Elmo. He explained that ore cars were lifted by a pulley system up an elevator shaft and dumped high overhead onto a belt called a tipple. The tipple fed the ore into a hopper bin where it dropped, with a little help from gravity, into a mortar box.

After that, a stamp battery pulverized the ore from the mortar box into a fine pulp. The pulp from the crushed ore was splashed against copper screens where some of the gold nuggets were recovered from the screens, and the rest of the pulp was washed with water, mercury and cyanide to eat away the dirt.

The now refined pulp was allowed to run slowly over a series of inclined copper plates where the larger pieces of gold were retained from the plates. The remaining gold amalgam was then squeezed through filter bags to separate the chemicals out and smelted to get the finer pieces of gold out of the mixture. Unfortunately, the mercury and sludge were released into the water, where it had flowed downstream and into the ground water.

The lower part of the mountain was still fractured, pitted with holes and mine shafts that were never mapped so one could easily step in the wrong place and fall into an unseen abyss. Down near the mill it was still dangerous one hundred years after the fact, and only the upper part of the property was deemed safe. This area was where Ray had decided a museum was going to be built.

Ray and Lugenia had planned to tear down the old mill, improve the road to the Sleeping Abe and build a museum of hand-cut sandstone from an old building they had torn down and salvaged in Sturgis.

The Crawfords had collected numerous antiques: furniture, gemstones, mining paraphernalia, and many other interesting artifacts throughout their lives, and they needed a place to display them. They were both history buffs and realized much of the mining they had done needed to be categorized and catalogued. They felt that the artifacts and photographs needed to be displayed for others to enjoy in the future.

Painfully, Jillian recalled how on the thirteenth of June in 1976, her father, Avery Moore, was clearing ground up on the Sleeping Abe for the foundation of the museum when the track broke on the Caterpillar he was operating. The Cat flipped over and rolled into a shallow ravine, killing him immediately. He was 43 years old. In July, Jillian's mother left her children with the Crawfords and never felt the need to come back for them.

Ray never finished his dream. Instead, he died of a heart attack in the spring of 1978. Unable to handle all of the stress and responsibility,

Lugenia closed the lodge and sold the campground, cheaply, to a group of investors, unknown to Jillian or Aunt Carla.

Coming back to the present, Jillian realized a large cloud has covered the sun and she was getting cold. She rushes back to the lodge to help her girls wait on customers and get ready for her date.

Chapter 8
The Truth Revealed

Jillian, having returned to the apartment, started a fire and curled up on the couch with Aunt Carla sitting beside her. A pot of coffee sitting on the table in front of them released steam wistfully into the air.

"So tell me, how was your trip, Aunt Carla?" Jillian inquired as she poured a cup of the steaming liquid into two of Grandma's antique rose patterned cups.

"Just fine dear, it went fast," Carla responded as she held her cup in the air. "I haven't seen these in a very long time."

"I've been kind of lost in the past for some reason and when I noticed these in the hutch I couldn't help but get them out and use them," Jillian replied. "Your mother did love roses, didn't she, Aunt Carla?"

"Yes, Jillian, she did."

"So tell me, what's up? Where is Jennifer and why didn't she come along this trip? I was expecting her to be along with you, not Heath Connors!"

"You know Jennifer would have loved to have brought her family, but Tom had to go to Florida so they went along. They're taking the kids to Disney World instead. She said to be sure to tell you hello."

Jillian liked her cousin Jennifer; she was three years younger than her and as beautiful as her aunt had been when she was younger, with black hair and beautiful skin.

"Maybe she can slip out next year if she misses me too much. Besides, I wouldn't turn down a trip to a theme park for anything. I love theme parks," Jillian replied.

Aunt Carla took pictures of Jennifer's four children out of her purse and handed them to Jillian. After more small talk, a serious expression overtook Carla's face and Jillian wondered what was on her mind.

"Jillian, what do you think Ian is going to do with the Sleepinb Abe property? He acts as though he has forgotten about it or pretends it doesn't exist. It certainly seems like a waste for it to just sit there and not use it."

"Gosh, I don't know for sure, Ian does own it after all. Even if he doesn't seem to care that much about it, I think deep down he has strong emotional ties to it," Jillian replied, surprised at the question.

"Well, I was wondering if he would consider selling it to me," Aunt Carla asked as she twirled a thread on Jillian's afghan, the same afghan she and Heath had cuddled up in together years before on the Sleeping Abe. She couldn't make herself put it away.

"Would you like me to ask him the next time I talk to him? I know he had talked about selling it in the past but with the state that place is in, I think he just figured no one would want to incur the cost of cleaning it up," Jillian answered.

"I don't think I have the money right now, Jillian, but perhaps we can save enough in the future. I just don't want him to sell it to someone else while I am trying to raise the funds. It could take me some time." Aunt Carla turned away from Jillian and stared into the warm, glowing fireplace. Jillian detected a forlorn, far away look in her aunt's face that she didn't quite understand.

"I can call Ian for you and find out what he wants to do. If he does want to sell, I can ask him what he wants for it," Jillian promised.

"That would be fine, Jillian, I would appreciate it if you would talk to him for me," Aunt Carla replied, still in a detached manner.

Jillian wondered what she was planning but decided it was best not to pursue it any farther and instead chose to change the subject.

"Heath has asked me out tonight, what do think about that?" she asked her aunt so lightheartedly it surprised her to hear her own voice.

Aunt Carla gave Jillian a knowing grin and said, "He still cares about you, you know. Heath's ex-wife was spoiled rotten. She gave him nothing but grief. He's talked to Jake about her over the years, so we knew quite a bit about what went on between them. After his divorce, he seemed quite determined that he was going to see you again. We didn't know how you would react to us bringing him along, unannounced and all. I hope you're not upset at me for letting him come."

Undoubtedly Jillian had felt rather agitated this morning when they had first arrived but right now she felt an excitement growing within her that she didn't want to acknowledge just yet. She found that she couldn't tell her aunt the extent of her feelings for Heath because she didn't even know what they were at this juncture.

"No, I'm not upset at you at all. He could have given me some kind of warning though; it's not exactly proper protocol to just show up on a person's doorstep without some kind of forewarning," she reasoned.

"Be patient with him, Jillian, he's really a very good guy. Go have some fun together, see what happens."

"I'll keep that in mind," Jillian said. "However, since I'm going on my first date in this century, heck for that matter this millennia, that sounds bad doesn't it? Anyway, there are hamburger patties, buns and potato salad in the walk in, so please feel free to cook and eat anything you want. Mi casa es su casa, as they say."

"Thanks sweetie, have a good time. By the way, did I hear you say you're going to Flintstones Village? What's the deal? You could have gone to any restaurant in the hills and you picked there? Why?"

"Heck, I don't know Aunt Carla, it just sounded like fun. I don't get to just be silly and have fun very often and I'm in a restaurant all the time, so that just didn't sound too appealing I guess."

"Oh! That makes sense, though I never would have thought of it. I personally prefer to be wined and dined, as they say." She laughed offhandedly and then took a sip of hot coffee. Jillian excused herself and headed toward the bathroom to get ready. For what, she didn't know.

Jillian took a shower, using a bath gel she had bought about a year ago but had never had an occasion to use. She blew her hair dry and took extra time applying her make-up. She always admonished herself to shop for make-up but never did, and now realized her mascara was dangerously out of date.

Nervously waiting to hear from Heath, she fidgeted with the lint build up in her blow dryer, wondering if he said 6:00 or 6:30. *This is as good as it gets*, she thought as she gave her hair a quick spray of Aqua Net.

Her cell phone rang. She practically broke her leg trying to locate it.

"Hey Betty, what time are we expected for dinosaur ribs at the Flintstones?" he jokingly asked her.

"Well, I'm just about ready, Barney, at least I will be when my leg quits hurting," she replied rubbing her shin, "but, didn't you say you would pick me up at six?"

"Actually, I was so tense I can hardly even remember what I said. Are my kids supposed to come with us or are we old enough to go by ourselves?" he inquired.

Jillian rolled her eyes, knowing full well that he would find a way to be alone with her, one way or another.

"Listen, if they want to come along that would be great, but if not they can hang out here at the lodge and explore the area. It's totally up to them," she retorted, already knowing his answer was not going to include his kids.

"They think they're too old for the Pebbles and Bam Bam thing, so if you don't mind hanging out with me in Bedrock I will come get you in a few minutes." Heath was mocking her, she could hear it, but she relented to his offer of spending the evening with just him.

"Oh, by the way, how did you get my cell phone number?" Jillian asked.

"Uh, well, actually I got it from your aunt's phone last night in Rapid City. I snooped through her numbers when she was brushing her teeth in the bathroom. Bad habit of mine, being snoopy. Sorry, I hope you're not mad."

"You know the old saying, sweetheart: I don't get mad, I get even."

"Ouch!" he howled. "On my honor, I will behave from this day forward and never give you a reason to get even."

"Do you promise?"

"I promise. We're on our way," he announced and they ended the conversation. Within fifteen minutes he and the kids pulled up in front of the lodge. They got out and sat politely on the front porch as if the whole family was nervous about Dad's big date tonight.

"Hey, everybody!" Jillian called out. "I'm amazed that you found anywhere to stay; this is the Independence Day weekend, you know." She looks at Heath and batted her eyelashes. "Most people make reservations about a year in advance. How did you pull this one off?"

"I was standing at the counter of the Super 8, begging like a puppy for food, when out of the blue someone from Iowa called in and canceled their reservation right in front of me. Now that sweet lady at the counter could see my poor family was in distress and couldn't help but offer the room to us. Right kids?"

"Yeah right, Dad, whatever," Kaitlyn said as she rolled her eyes up and around, causing everyone to break out in laughter at her.

"I have a guardian angel, Jillian, her name is Harriet," he teased. "She watches out for me and the kids, and on rare occasions finds us motel rooms on the spur of the moment."

"Oh, Harriet is it? How interesting." Jillian chuckled. "You are full of it, mister. Are you about ready to go?"

Jillian gave instructions to Jake for the kids to stay off of the Sleeping Abe but they could hike a little way up the Sunday Gulch trail if they wanted too.

"Don't go too far in the dark, there are mountain lions and bob cats in them thar' hills," she teased. "Seriously, take the walkie-talkies beside my bed if you are going anywhere up in the trees. People get lost in the woods here all the time, so don't risk it, please? Bye, love you."

"Bye Dad, bye Jillian," Kaitlyn sang out.

Heath opened the door for her and she climbed into his SUV.

Waving to the smiling crowd they pull around the horse shoe and headed toward the amusement park in Custer. She noticed that Heath was grinning like the Cheshire cat.

"What?" Jillian finally got up the nerve to ask him. "What are you smiling at?"

"My goodness girl, you look beautiful, just like I had you pictured from the last time I saw you, Jillian. It's hard for me to believe I'm actually in the presence of your company again."

"Really, and you had how long to prepare for this, shall we say, reunion?"

"I made the decision to come on the spur of the moment. Jake mentioned to me about three weeks ago that everyone was coming to South Dakota so I asked about you and I realized I had to see you again."

Feeling troubled by his candid comment, she decided it was way past time to clear the stale air between them.

"Pull over, Heath, we need to talk."

Heath, fully expecting this reaction, welcoming it even, pulled onto a side road as far from oncoming traffic as he could. He turned sideways to look at her. "What's on your mind, Jillian?" he asked, anticipating a thorough interrogation.

"For starters, why don't you explain to me why you didn't contact me when you went back to California and why after all these years you have suddenly decided to come back here? I want the truth, Heath, what's going on?"

Looking guilty, Heath began to explain. "I had a fiancé when I met you, Jillian, an arrangement our parents had made at the country club. I didn't love her the way I knew I should. She turned out to be selfish, refusing to let me touch her. She didn't care for our children. We were married for 15 years, some of it was good," he explained in a melancholy tone. "Then she acquired a boyfriend from the preppy group she was fond of hanging out with and I filed for divorce. It's been hard on my kids. She didn't want custody, and it made them feel like they were just a big imposition to her."

Jillian knew instinctively what that feeling was like; her own mother had given her a taste of it when she was young. *It was that gift that kept on giving,* she thought.

She replied softly, "You rejected me, Heath. I gave my heart to you and you walked away from me just like she did to you. What am I supposed to think? You knew that I loved you. You said that you loved me too, but that didn't seem to matter because you left me and you didn't come back. You hurt me. You hurt me more than you will ever know."

Jillian began to feel hot, stinging tears well up in her eyes.

"I am sorry, Jillian." Heath put his hand to the side of her cheek and turned her face gently toward his. "Please, forgive me for lying to you. I was afraid of my parents, afraid of what they would do if I backed out of the wedding. I wanted you, Jillian, you were the one, I knew it, but I wasn't man enough to stand up to my parents and call it off. I'm not that kid anymore. I won't let you go this time and I mean that. I will never lie to you again, I promise."

Allowing him to brush his lips up the side of her cheek and to gently kiss the lobe of her ear she whispered, "You need to drive, Heath, this is going way to fast for me right now."

Heath, feeling aroused, took a deep breath, straightened up in his seat and pulled carefully out on to the highway. They continued to drive the last 10 miles toward Custer in silence.

Their subdued mood began to lighten as they entered Flintstone Village. Barney and Fred were walking around the park, so they talked another tourist into taking their picture with the two characters. Heath bought Ryan and Kaitlyn tee shirts from the gift shop. While riding the train around the park they ate cotton candy. They ordered brontosaurus burgers from the drive-in and shared a banana split. When it was time to go, Heath suggested they stop for a drink at the Captain's Table nearby. Jillian has never had a night quite like this in her whole life and felt painfully aware of what she had been missing out on these last twenty years by not letting a man into her life.

At midnight they pull up in front of the lodge. Her aunt and uncle were sitting in the dark on the porch talking in low voices. They were having a serious conversation about something, but as Jillian and

Heath walked up to them they become curiously quiet.

"Looks like you two had a good time," Uncle Victor said.

"We did," Heath replied, looking at his date, "we did."

Heath and Jillian entered her apartment and quietly observed all four of the kids sprawled out, two on the bed, one on the couch and one on the floor watching a movie.

Jillian sucked in her breath at the perfectness of the picture in front of her. Burning embers in the rock fireplace cast shadows on the log walls of the old building, illuminating the peaceful faces of the teenagers. She thought poignantly that not having children was the one thing in life she had missed the most.

Chapter 9
The Thing

In the still of the night, Jillian once again dreamed of the past. The stress and excitement of the long day must have opened a window from her subconscious mind into her world of dreams and daydreams. Many family issues were hidden in there, always lurking under a façade of nice words and pleasantries.

She didn't know whether Aunt Carla's visit or her reunion with Heath has opened this window. Maybe she just needed to remember the events of the past so that she could forgive the worst of the cast members, get the hell out of limbo, and move on with her life.

But tonight, she replayed the distant events in her mind as if they had just happened yesterday. She tossed from side to side as she fell deeply into a restless sleep. The changeover came easily, as if stepping through a door, a portal maybe, to the day Grandpa Ray died.

It was 1978 all over again. Jillian could feel that she was filled to the brim with youth. The smell of fall was just beginning to fill the air with its musky scent. The aspen and birch trees were still a pale green, but soon would transition into iridescent leaves of gold like a fine Persian rug.

The little black and white spotted trees with the paper thin white bark grew on the sides of the steepest slopes, in a slow, steady march to the top of the mountain, competing for space and sun in the predominately pine and spruce forest. She lived in an ecosystem fighting to stay in balance.

This dazzling fall display comes on quickly, staying for only a couple of weekends. Then, the first Canadian cold front will come barreling across the plains, slamming into the hills and dumping deep piles of snow on the locals and whatever tourists are still remaining. The winters always felt so blasted long to her, with short days and cold temperatures.

Jillian felt the potential of this day, a Saturday, sweeping her up in a bundle of unbridled enthusiasm. She knew perfect days like that were short lived and made plans to enjoy the last of the nice weather.

She and Karen had made plans to drive into Rapid City to meet Ian today. They were going to finish up the last of their school shopping, eat an early supper at the Pizza Barrel, and then see this scary new movie *Alien*. They planned to sleep on the floor in Ian's new apartment tonight, and if they were lucky, Ian might buy them some Miller Light Beer.

She and Karen were seniors that year at Hill City High and Ian was a sophomore at the Black Hills School of Mines and Technology. Life was good for her. No, not just good, but so full of exciting plans for the future it was difficult to contain the joy she was feeling.

"Grandma, I need a pair of new Converse tennis shoes for volleyball this year and I'm going to need some knee pads too."

"What's wrong with the pair you had last year?" Grandma asked from the bedroom.

"They're worn out. I really do need a new pair for this year. I have forty dollars of my allowance left; if it comes to more than that will you help me? I'll do extra chores, I promise."

"Of course we'll help you pay for it, Jillian," Grandpa boomed behind her, surprising her as he came in the back door of the old house.

"Grandpa, you scared me! I thought you were up on the Sleeping Abe this morning?" She walked over and gave him a quick peck on the cheek.

"I was but I got tired, think I'll take a little nap," he replied.

Jillian remembered thinking that was an unusual statement coming from him, he had always been strong and robust, but lately he has seemed more tired than usual.

"Are you feeling okay, Grandpa? Grandpa? Oh God! Grandma! Grandma come in here, something's wrong."

She witnessed the chilling scene unfolding in front of her. She felt as though she was floating above it, just watching, like a bystander. Grandpa Crawford, clutching his chest, fell to the floor, dying slowly as she and Grandma stood by helplessly, not knowing CPR or even what to do.

"Sudden Cardiac Death" was its official name, but she preferred to think that Grandpa had died of a broken heart over the loss of her dad, his stepson, Avery. Grandma had said that he felt responsible for that tractor malfunctioning like it did, but no one had ever cast any blame toward him. He buried himself in guilt, nonetheless.

She felt acutely aware of how drastically life had changed for her and Ian since that awful day. Nothing even resembled their life with Ray Crawford any more. He was a hero in her mind, saving her grandmother, her father, and Carla back in the late '30s and her and Ian in the mid '70s. He was the cement, the glue that held them all together and without that glue, she remembered in horror, how Grandma began to fall apart.

Only weeks after Grandpa's funeral, even before the snow began to fly that year, Grandma began to make excuses to Jillian that she was going to the store, or to the Senior Center, or the beauty shop, and not coming home at night. Shortly thereafter she closed up the lodge, sold the campground ridiculously cheap, and retired.

Carla was very upset at her because her family was to inherit the campground when her mother passed away, it said so in her stepfather's will. It didn't say anything about selling it out from under her nose. Grandma had given the money to Carla but it was nothing, only a pittance of its true value.

Victor and Carla tried to talk some sense into her but she wouldn't listen. "It's my life and my money and I'll do whatever I damn well please with both of them, now butt out," she announced abruptly.

"I'm getting a lawyer, Mom; I just want you to know that we are going to contest the sale of campground on the grounds that you are no longer competent."

"You do what you have to do, Carla, but you won't find the new owners, I guarantee it." Grandma shook up everyone with that declaration and as far as Jillian knew, the Jordans didn't follow through on their threat.

Now the question remained, who had she sold the campground to? People came to run it but they were not the owners and were mighty tight lipped about who they were working for. A group of investors was the pat answer, nothing more.

Roseanne Sanderson finally told Jillian that Lugenia Crawford had been seen in town hanging around some low-life alcoholic that is at least a decade younger than her. She was at the bars with him getting drunk.

"He's trouble, Jillian," Roseanne had said, and Jillian could still feel how embarrassed she was by it.

All she knew about this guy was that he was an old prospector who dabbled in gold mining, but was usually unemployed and down on his luck. He drank too much and had taken up residence at the sleaziest bar in town. Lugenia, being a wealthy widow, distraught over the death of her husband and only son, seemed like such an easy target for unscrupulous thugs such as him.

Jillian remembered her dismay, when, in the early spring of 1979, Grandma moved him into the old house with them lock, stock and barrel. His name was Bert, and Jillian hated him from the onset. Reliving the scene, she watches as he acted sickeningly sweet to her in front of her grandma but made lewd passes at her when Grandma was not within earshot.

"Come here, Jillian, set on my lap and let me rub your back for you." His haunting voice echoed in her ears as he laughed at her, grabbing and groping at her.

"Leave me alone," she said aloud, waking Jake in the back bedroom.

Jake listened for anymore outbursts from her but heard only heavy breathing from all the sleeping bodies in this small apartment. He's not sleeping very soundly, never does anymore, especially on an unfamiliar mattress.

Continuing to dream, she smelled the whiskey and tobacco on Bert's breath, and wrinkled up her nose at his brown, rotting teeth. The filth on his clothes only added to her disgust. He was by all accounts repulsive and Jillian knew he has the capacity to hurt her if he got the notion.

Jillian, at eighteen, made a decision to stay in town with the Sandersons just to avoid having to see him altogether and she can not, for the life of her, figure out what her grandmother saw in this sorry character.

Continuing deeper into her dream, Jillian recalled hearing Grandma proudly exclaiming to her and Ian, "Bert and I went shopping for just a few small pieces of equipment today. Bert wants to do some placer mining up on the Sleeping Abe."

What Grandma brought home was a front-end loader, a used scraper and all of the equipment Bert needed to begin his little endeavor. Pricy goods to be sure.

Ian and Jillian were concerned. Their grandma had been acting strangely, spending money on Bert like it grew on trees and bragging about it to anyone who would listen. Her friends, of whom she once had many, began to stay away, wondering if she had not totally lost her marbles altogether.

It was Bert who convinced Lugenia there was still enough gold at the Sleeping Abe to justify placer mining. After she agreed to his ridiculous plan he set about building a contraption to do just that. He built a large, noisy, smoke-belching machine where dirt from the ground was dumped onto a screen called a shaker. The sifted dirt from the shaker fell into a box that water ran over. Since gold weighs more than the dirt, the gold settled into the bottom of the shaker box where Bert recovered it by panning it out by hand. The whole contraption was ugly. Jillian hated how shabby it made the property look, not to mention the fact that he was wreaking havoc with the environment up there by digging holes, uprooting the natural grasses and tearing down small trees.

"Don't go, Ian, he's trying to kill you," Jillian mumbled aloud as her dream turned to a time even darker and scarier.

55

She watched helplessly as Bert led Ian into the old mill that was on the verge of collapsing, convincing Ian that he had shored up the rafters to make it safe even though he hadn't. Bert had Ian exploring the old mining tunnels under the elevator shaft which were dripping with water, rotting the supporting timbers below and threatening to cave in at a moment's notice. Ian, oblivious to any danger, seemed to enjoy the attention, but Jillian knew Bert was up to no good.

Bert had never produced much gold from the property, though gold prices were sky-rocketing, yet he spent a lot of time up on the Sleeping Abe digging holes and filling them in with the dirt he had taken from the next hole he dug.

"What is he doing?" she whispered into the night. "What is he looking for?"

Jillian found her elf begging Ian not to go up to the Sleeping Abe with Bert any more. She suspected that Bert was trying to hurt him, but why? Ian owned the Sleeping Abe, that's why! It had to be, because Ian could stop him from insanely digging all those holes. Even if Ian didn't get full ownership of the Sleeping Abe until his grandma passed on, he was still in Bert's way.

Ian couldn't help himself, he was studying geology, and being able to walk right into the side of a mountain, regardless of its stability, was just too enticing. None of his classmates owned their own gold mine like he did. It was his own personal laboratory and on more than one occasion it had helped him with research on his homework.

Changing directions, Jillian's mind wandered to her best friend Karen. Jillian had met Karen the summer of 1978, when they came here on vacation from Missouri. They had camped for two weeks at the campground and liked it so much that they decided to move into Hill City. When Grandpa died a short time later, Roseanne had helped out by bringing food to the reception after the funeral, even though she didn't really know him all that well.

In April of 1979, realizing that Jillian was struggling with her grandmother's new boyfriend, Roseanne invited her to move to town and stay with them. She did so gladly.

Jillian can see her self studying at Roseanne's kitchen table, trying to keep her grades up amidst the chaos running rampant around her.

Roseanne had taken such good care of her during that time, attending her volleyball games, including Jillian in a big graduation bash she threw for Karen, and most of all cooking for her. She appreciated it so much that she had Roseanne out to the Silver Belle Lodge for supper, on the house, at least once a month since she first opened the place, to try to return the favor.

Remembering Bert once again, Jillian thought back to when she first began to notice her grandmother's behavior turning from just plain silly to irrational. It was May, only one month after she had moved out. *Maybe I should have stayed so I could have kept an eye on things*, she thought. *This is partly my fault for leaving her.* She watched herself frantically telling Aunt Carla, "She seems to be getting sicker with each passing week, you must come, I need help with her."

Jillian remembered the putrid smell of vomit leading her to the bathroom in the lodge where one evening she found Grandma laying on the floor, too weak to hold her head up any longer.

"How did you get over here? Where is Bert?" Jillian asked her in a panic, running back to the house to call for help.

Her panic rose as Jillian called for an ambulance. On the way to the hospital Grandma kept repeating, "The pink rose; Jillian, look for the pinkest rose," and later that night Jillian watched helplessly as her grandmother died in the emergency room at the hospital in Rapid City. Crying hysterically, Jillian just did not know what to make of it and ordered bouquets of pink roses for her funeral.

Wisely, the county coroner ordered an autopsy. The diagnosis was murder.

Lugenia Crawford tested positive for mercury and cyanide. It was assumed by them and law enforcement officials that Bert had found the lethal chemicals up on the Sleeping Abe mine and administered them to Lugenia, systematically poisoning her to death, with his motive being her money.

She thought back to the day he was handcuffed and taken into custody for the death of her grandmother and she felt hatred for him as if it happened only yesterday. She watched the gavel fall as the jury pronounced him guilty, guilty of only third degree murder, and sentenced him to prison for ten years. Usually a poisoning death was an automatic first degree sentence because it is premeditated, but Bert had only gotten the lesser charge and she never could figure out why the jury did that.

Jillian felt intense disappointment again, remembering his death in the winter of 1981, hoping he would have had to sit there for a long, long time. Jillian wanted him to pay for the agony he had caused her family. For what, she wondered?

He said he was innocent up to the day he died but she knew better, he did it.

"Why? Why did he do it?" she yelled aloud, yet still deep in sleep.

Her grandmother had always been overly generous with him and Jillian couldn't figure out why he needed more.

Everything up on the Sleeping Abe remained as it was on the day that Bert was taken into custody, causing Jillian anxiety. Ian had cleaned up some of Grandpa's materials for the museum but the front-end loader, the scraper, and the placer mining contraption were still up there. "It's a testament to Bert's greediness," Jillian told Karen and Roseanne.

Roseanne advised, "Why don't you have it dumped into the old mine shaft and pile the mill on top of it? It would eventually settle into the hole and you would kill two birds with one stone that way."

"No!" Ian said when she approached him with the idea. And that was that.

Continuing, Jillian saw herself and Aunt Carla at the auction they held for the antiques that Grandpa had intended to display in the museum. She saw people coming from every direction, buying the old furniture, antique rugs, railroad antiques, photographs, books, glassware and gemstones her grandparents had spent thirty years collecting.

"Stop!" she yelled loudly, "That belongs to us! Stop it, stop it now!"

"Jillian, wake up," Jake said as he shook her awake. "You're having a bad dream."

"Oh, I'm sorry, did I wake everyone up?" she asked sleepily.

"It's okay Jillian, go back to sleep," Jake replied as he covered her up. "Tomorrow is a new day."

Chapter 10
Sight-seeing

July 3, the day before Independence Day, dawned brightly, promising to be a day of pure splendor for touring through the Hills. Knowing it was a lot to ask, Jillian had bribed Karen and Roxie to pinch-hit for her over the weekend. Playing tour guide for her family sounded like such fun that she offered both her employees a nice bonus if they would work. Fortunately, Karen had said she would cook and Roxie had said she would wait tables.

That morning Karen unexpectedly showed up at work with a strange little guy that she introduced to everyone as Jon Harden. She seemed rather smitten with him and Jillian thought it seemed a little out of character for her.

He's not her type, Jillian thought, as she had never seen Karen with anyone as vertically challenged as this little man was.

"My car broke down. But Jon was sweet enough to give me a ride; he's such a nice guy," Karen gushed.

This unusual looking stranger greeted everyone warmly, asked for a glass of iced tea and proceeded to make himself quite at home with her family.

"What do you do for a living, Jon?" Heath asked politely.

"I drive a lumber truck for a logging company in Rapid City. I work all over the Hills, depending on the day and location," he volunteered.

Jillian couldn't help but be amazed at the fact he could reach the petals, let alone drive the truck.

"You drive a lumber truck?" she asked, trying hard not to be rude. It just didn't seem possible with his diminutive size.

"I have my own truck, designed especially for me, and I contract out to lumber companies," he clarified.

"Well, it's nice to meet you, Jon," Jillian said. "Now, if you will all excuse Karen and me, we have work to do in the kitchen."

Karen and Jillian headed into the lodge to proceed with the changing of the guards. Jillian couldn't wait. Curiosity had gotten the better of her and she had to know what the skinny was on Karen's miniature man.

"Where did you meet that guy, Karen?" she questioned. "He doesn't seem like your type at all."

"What? You don't like him?" Karen retorted, giving Jillian a smirk.

"That's not fair; that's not what I said and you answered my question with another question. Me first! Now, where did you meet that guy?"

"Okay, okay! My mom introduced him to me. His mom, Alexis Harden, and my mom are friends, so of course they thought we should hook up. He's been an absolute sweetheart to me though, Jillian. I know he's kinda short, but so what?"

"So what nothin'! As long as he's taking care of my friend, that's all that matters to me."

"He is, so don't worry. So who's the tall, tan and handsome guy you went out with last night?" Karen asked bluntly, catching Jillian completely off guard with the question.

Jillian, trying unsuccessfully to stifle a smile, broke into laughter. "How did you know about that?"

"Okay, so who's answering with a question now?"

"That's too bad, Karen! How did you know I was with someone last night?"

"Oh, you know me; I've got friends in low places. They saw you at the bar in Custer," she replied offhandedly.

"Great! I haven't been the subject of idle gossip in ages, feels kind of good actually." She winked at Karen. "You remember Heath

Connors, don't you? He's that guy that came out here from California with my cousins back in 1985?" Jillian asked sheepishly.

"Oh my God, Jillian, that's him? That guy you were with last night is him? Jillian, you more than just liked him girl, you were head over heals in love with him," Karen said excitedly, grabbing her shoulders.

"Shh….he's out on the porch, and besides, I was not in love with him," Jillian retorted indignantly, pulling away.

"Like heck you weren't. You can fool some of the people some of the time, sweetheart, but you're not fooling me. Don't forget, I was here when he left. You moped around like a lost puppy for months," Karen replied.

"Was I really that bad?" Jillian asked her friend.

"Pretty bad," Karen replied.

"Hey, thanks for working today, Karen," Jillian said, quickly hugging her friend and effectively changing the subject away from that tumultuous time in her life.

"No problem sister, go, have a good time," Karen said supportively. "Jon is going to do dishes for awhile and keep me company. Is that okay with you, boss?"

"That's fine. Any help we can round up is a good thing out here, especially on a holiday weekend. Now if you need something, I'll have my cell phone," Jillian replied and headed into the walk-in to retrieve the sandwiches she had made for the trip that day.

"Goodbye Roxie, take care of this crazy cook for me, okay?" Jillian saids over her shoulder,

"Will do, Miss Jillian," Roxie drawled in her west Texas accent.

Jillian knew that Roxie had met a South Dakota bull rider at the Ranch Rodeo Championship in her hometown of Amarillo, Texas. She followed him north, had two of his kids and then he hit the road again, leaving her behind. When her divorce was final, she intended on heading back to Texas but for now she needed to work, and Jillian was happy to have her for however long she stayed.

Still wondering about Jon Harden, Jillian packed a cooler and wondered where he's from and how he got here. Trying to recall if she had ever met anyone named Alexis Harden, she found that the name meant nothing to her. *Oh well*, she thought, *I have better things to concern myself with at the moment and he is waiting for me out front.* The thought made her giddy as she opened the screen door and practically bopped out to the porch.

"Have fun, Jillian," Karen yelled out the door behind her.

Jillian, Heath and his two kids were touring in the black SUV. Jake and Cindy and their two kids were following in the mini van. They took the walkie-talkies so the kids could talk back and forth as they drove.

Standing on the front porch of the lodge, the family made final plans.

"What are you and Uncle Victor going to do today?" Jillian inquired.

"We don't have anything definite going on yet. We'll probably just tootle through the Hills and maybe end up in Rapid and shop," Carla replied.

"You know you're more than welcome to come with us, Mom," Cindy interjected.

"No thank you, you kids go have some fun," she teased. "We old folks couldn't possibly keep up with you."

With Heath, Jillian, Ryan and Kaitlyn leading the pack, the entourage headed toward Mt. Rushmore. Jillian takes her followers on a breathtaking cut across called the Palmer Creek Road. Mostly unknown to tourist, the locals had been using this winding, dirt road for years to skirt the busy junction down below that intersects the Gutzon Borglum Memorial Highway and the road into Hill City.

First, one winds through an aspen and birch forest, emerging suddenly into a lovely little two mile long meadow. The meadow is lush, with a trout–filled little creek that provides a cool drink for the horses, deer and elk. On your right flank is a one thousand foot sheer wall of granite majestically supporting the lookout tower of Harney Peak. Jillian wants to share this place, her favorite place in the Hills, with Heath's family.

"Heath, pull over, you need to stop and look at this," she said persuasively.

Spellbound at the magnitude of the rock face and the sweet smell of the wild flowers, Heath knew instantly why Jillian felt drawn to this magical meadow. He took her hand and together they scanned the area for wildlife. Up near the peak they see two white dots—mountain goats hanging precariously from their tiny footholds.

Next, they intersect the highway, take a right turn and head up the Gutzon Borglum Memorial Highway toward Mount Rushmore. For the next two hours they visit the presidents, take pictures and explore the monument. Heath buys more tee-shirts.

Jake is stunned. "When did all of this happen?" he asked, sweeping his arm around the area, indicating his astonishment at the changes made in the late '90s when the entire façade of Mt. Rushmore was redone.

"What do you think of it?" Jillian asked him cautiously.

"I think it was fine the way it was," he exclaimed. "It looks Greek, like the Parthenon or the Acropolis."

"That's what I thought at first, but I actually like it because it is very user friendly now. The traffic is so heavy up here anymore that they needed to do something.

"I suppose you're right, but it will take some getting used too," Jake said dejectedly. "I swear, if I hadn't seen the faces in the background I wouldn't have known where I was."

"You can't stop progress, Jake; can you imagine what everyone must have thought when they first started carving this? I remember Grandpa saying that his friends thought it was the craziest thing they ever heard, now look at it. It really is quite a place, you gotta admit."

"It's just not the Mt. Rushmore of my youth is all, Jillian. I used to climb on the rocks, and run around here like it belonged to me. With all of this security it really doesn't feel like it's ours anymore, it belongs to Uncle Sam."

"It always belonged to Uncle Sam, sweetheart; he just used to trust everyone before September eleventh. This security is necessary; you should know that. Yosemite is the same way, isn't it?"

"Yup, it's the same way. Sad, isn't it?"

"Yup, it's sad that we have to take precautions like this. It certainly is."

Around noon the group careened down the mountainside into Keystone to find something to eat. The Ruby House, a quaint restaurant on the boardwalk, was a welcome oasis to have an iced tea and watch the bustling little tourist town kick into action. Brian headed across the street to buy old fashioned salt water taffy and the other three teens followed.

"Are you tired yet?" Jillian asked Heath.

"Good heavens, no! We just got started!" Excitedly, he exclaimed, "What do you think about us getting our picture taken at that old fashioned photographer over there?"

"No," Jillian stated emphatically.

"Yes," he retorted, raising his eyebrows at her. "I want a picture with you sitting on my lap in a sexy barmaid outfit."

"I'll bet you do," she laughed. "Okay, just this once."

While Heath and Jillian prepared for their picture, Jake and Cindy wandered through some of the shops nearby. Jake bought his bride a Black Hills gold ring with a beautiful opal in the center.

"Can we ride on the 1880 Train, Dad?" Brian asked.

"Absolutely," Jake replied. Taking Cindy's hand, he felt happier than he had in many years. It was so nice to be here.

When the picture was through, Jillian took her guests on the old road, watching as the Old Number 7 engine chugged its way back down the pass from Keystone toward Hill City, with the winding road crossing the track over and over again.

At each crossing the engineer would pull on the whistle, unleashing a blast of steam through the chamber that gave each little engine its own signature sound. She recognized each whistle and whether it was coming to or leaving Hill City.

"Did you know that they make this trip about four times a day?" Jillian asked, wanting to let Heath in on her love of steam engines.

"Really, you seem to know quite a bit about this place, are you over here a lot?" Heath questioned her.

"Not anymore, but my dad worked for the railroad all of his life and he taught Ian and I all about trains," she replied matter-of-factly. "For instance, did you know that a steam engine is classified according to

65

its wheel configuration, such as a two-six-zero being a Mogul?"

"No, I can't say that I knew that. What does a two-six-zero mean?"

"It means that first there are two small pilot trucks in the front, and then six larger drivers in the middle and finally, zero dolly wheels under the firebox. Each type of locomotive has a nickname according to its wheel configuration such as the two-six-two being a Prairie, a four-six-two being a Pacific, or a four-six-four being a Hudson."

"Wow, that's cool, I didn't know that," he exclaimed. "Do you like train travel?"

Jillian sighed, "Let's just say my biggest fantasy is to take one year and travel on as many trains as I can find, beginning with the American Orient Express. I love train travel, I can't help it; it reminds me of my childhood. My father would get coach tickets for a discount so we would travel to Denver, Colorado, or up to Sheridan, Wyoming. We were still a nice little family back then, just riding the rails, happy as clams."

"We're going to miss the next train if we don't hurry," Jake cut in over the handheld radio. "We still have to buy tickets.

"Ten-four Good buddy, we are on our way to the 1880 train station to buy tickets," she said, causing Ryan and Kaitlyn to laugh.

Driving down the old road, Heath and Jillian find that they were easily conversant with each other, and also found themselves talking about everything under the sun.

"Tell me about your Aunt Carla, Jillian. I only know her from California but I'll bet she left quite an impression in South Dakota in her younger years. I'll bet she turned some heads in her day," Heath said.

"Oh yeah, I guess she was kind of wild from what I hear," Jillian replied. "My dad always said that she had her pick of boyfriends in high school but she ran off and eloped with Victor Jordan and stunned everyone, especially my grandma. He came to Edgemont because he got a job as a ranch hand and didn't have a penny to his name from what I hear. In 1955 they moved out west to California."

"Was she an accountant back then?" Heath asks.

"No, I think she earned her degree in tax accounting in California. She has been doing my books for a long time. Unfortunately, she knows how broke I am too," Jillian smiled.

Jillian sat quietly as Heath drove the winding path toward town. She let thoughts of her aunt run loosely through her mind. After Grandma was gone, it seemed that it took an army of lawyers to get her estate settled. Unfortunately, Jillian hadn't paid that much attention to the financial end of Grandma's affairs. Only being nineteen, she preferred to let Carla handle the details.

One particular afternoon in June her family sat in one of their offices, a formality really, to hear the last will and testament of Lugenia Crawford. She couldn't remember whose office anymore or even what the will said, but she did remember watching Carla irately pacing the floor.

"Where in the hell has my parent's money disappeared too!" she yelled at Victor. Fire flew from her green eyes as they went through her mother's final accounts. "There was money and now there isn't any, what did that good for nothing Bert do with it? What could he have possibly done with all the money Ray left to my mom?" She angrily shook a stack of receipts at everyone and walked out the door, slamming it soundly behind her.

Jillian didn't know what Carla was talking about because she had little actual knowledge of her grandparents' finances, but she never forgot the distress her aunt had displayed that day. Carla had never brought the subject up to Jillian again and Jillian was too afraid to ask her about it.

All Jillian knew was that none of them had received any money but each had gotten a nice piece of real estate. Carla got the campground; Ian got the Sleeping Abe and Jillian the lodge. She suspected that had Grandma not sold the campground, Carla could have easily retired from the money it consistently brought in every summer. It was easily the most lucrative property of the three and that is why Grandpa had given it to her, so she could share its profits with her children.

That evening, after a full day of touring and train rides, everyone congregated back at the lodge. Wanting to fish, the boys loaded their lines with worms and cast them into the pond. Ryan was the first to catch a fish, a two–pound trout, and then demonstrated how to clean it to the others. Jillian, impressed at his skill, let the kids fish until there was enough trout to feed everyone.

"Jillian, I don't like fish," Kaitlyn said in a shy tone. "Is there anything else I could eat?"

"Of course there is," Jillian replies. "How about a burger and fries?"

"Yeah, that would be great," Kaitlyn exclaimed as the two headed up to the kitchen, leaving the boys to fish.

Jillian, Carla and Cindy cheerfully set about preparing a meal that would have been fit for a king or at the very least, them. They ate together in the large dining room, ending their day with a succulent meal of grilled trout with peppered lemon butter, baked sweet potatoes with butter and brown sugar, homemade whole wheat bread and spinach salad with light balsamic vinaigrette. A bottle of Sauvignon Blanc filled Grandma's antique crystal stemware.

Cindy lit candles, rose-colored votives that were burning low on the pine tables giving an air of romance to the occasion. Jake brought in some pine logs and set about building a fire in the massive old rock fireplace. The smell of pine smoke wafted through the air, creating primordial memories of good food and love of family. Though Jillian seldom lit this fireplace, usually just on special occasions, this occasion felt pretty special in her mind.

"Did you and Uncle Victor enjoy your day, Aunt Carla?" Jillian asked.

Jake chimed in, "Yeah Mom, what did you old folks do to today, polish up your walkers?"

"Very funny son, no, we stayed close by. Let's see, first we drove up to Sylvan Lake, and then we drove up to the Needles. After that we came back here and took a nap."

"You need to see Mt. Rushmore, Mom, it's really changed. You and Dad should drive up there sometime this week and take a look at it." Jake continued, "I haven't decided whether I like it yet. Jillian is trying to convince me."

Finishing supper dishes, Jillian stood at the sink wondering if this budding relationship was the right thing to do. She secretly wished she could turn over a magic eight ball and simply get the correct answer. *Am I setting myself up to get hurt again?* she thought silently to herself.

Quietly, Heath snuck up behind her, wrapped his arms around her waist and asked in a seductive French accent, "Do you need any help, Cinderella?

"Thanks for the offer, but I'm just about done." She smiled back at him.

"Au contraire, mon friar." He gestured in a bowing motion. Using his best Pepe Le Pew voice, he immersed his hands into her sink of soapy water and said, "I did not offer to help you, madam, but only to find you help."

Heath playfully flicked water down Jillian's neck.

"I can't believe you just did that," she whimpered between gritted teeth. Pretending to be angry she declared, "Now you're gonna get it."

She retaliated by running her soapy hands down both sides of what she had long thought was his gorgeous face, and covered him from head to chin in a sudsy beard.

"Oh baby, I love it when you do that," he whispered seductively into her ear as he grabbed her, leaned her backward, and rubbed his soapy beard all over her face.

She screamed out loud, "You rat! I'm soaked."

Heath held her face and kissed her hard on her lips. His tongue found its way into her mouth as they wrapped their arms tightly around each other, trying to hold this perfect moment in time and not let it go. Water and soap soaked through their clothes but they didn't notice. Jillian knew she should make him stop but she didn't want him to stop—not anymore.

Heath sighed regretfully into her ear, "You have no idea how long I have wanted to do that. But I had better slow down before we get caught necking in the kitchen."

Guiding her out to the fireplace they stood together, letting the heat dry them off. The fire, the candles, and the darkness of the room were fueling a passionate flame between them. They stared intently into each other's eyes, knowing the desires of the other but not able to respond openly to it.

Jake too, noticed the atmosphere and moved some of the tables back. He puts Jillian's Bread CD on her stereo.

"Lovely wife," he teased Cindy, "would you like to dance?"

"Absolutely," she responded as they begin a slow waltz across the weathered pine floor. The old music reminded them all of a younger day.

"The finest years I ever knew, were all the years I had with you, and I would give every thing I own, I'd give up my life, my heart, my home, just to have you back again, just to touch you once again."

The lyrics made Jillian's cheeks burn hotly. Heath did not take his eyes off of her as they stood silently across from each other.

Startling Jillian back to reality, Heath abruptly stated, "Kids, it's getting late, we need to go."

Jillian suspected he had become aroused and needed to get away from her. She understood his need to leave. She knew there was a desire burning for him that she was having difficulty controlling herself.

"What would you like to do tomorrow?" Jillian asked him at the door as he was leaving.

"I'll leave that up to you, Jillian, you did a great job entertaining us today, thanks for supper. I'll call you tomorrow morning and we'll figure something out."

And without another word, he got in his vehicle and drove away.

Chapter 11
Kaitlyn's Surgery

Saturday morning came much too early for Jillian. Karen and Roxie came in to work at 10:00, and as usual Jillian had breakfast put away and the noon special ready to put into the oven. Today was the Fourth of July. Because St. Elmo's Silver Belle Lodge was located so near to Mt. Rushmore it usually was a very busy day for them.

"Good morning, how'd it go yesterday?" Jillian asked Karen as she came through the door.

"My gawd, we were swamped all day. Haven't you looked at the tickets yet?

"No, I'm too tired; it's going to have to wait. It was a good day, huh?" She hated to leave them yesterday but the time she had spent with Heath was so wonderful she didn't regret it, not for a minute.

"It was better than just a good day. We did about eighty tickets in eight hours and several of those tickets were eight or more people. My feet still hurt, not to mention my carpal tunnel problem."

"What carpal tunnel problem would that be?" Jillian asked, suspiciously eyeing her.

"Just kidding, you know I like sympathy. Jon stayed and washed dishes until he left for Hot Springs around two yesterday afternoon. We liked to have worked the poor guy to death. Oh yeah, I wanted to ask you, is your aunt moving to Hot Springs?" Karen asked out of the blue.

"No I don't think so, why do you ask?" Jillian countered.

"Well," Karen began, "Jon went to Hot Springs yesterday to get a wide load permit for his logging truck, he's logging over in Red Canyon next week, and he ran into your aunt coming out of the courthouse. He said hello to her but Jon said she was acting kind of strange, pretending she didn't know who he was, and for crying out loud, Jillian, she just met him yesterday!"

"Are you sure it was her?" she asked Karen, confused at the information.

"He was positive. He said she just gave him a little smile, looked right through him, and practically bolted for the door."

Jillian was deeply startled! Aunt Carla said they went up to Sylvan Lake, the Needles and then home for a nap. What were they doing clear over there? Hot Springs was at least 60 miles south of there and way out of her way.

"Which office did he see her in?" Jillian asked, wondering what her business was.

"Jon was leaving the Treasurers Office and she was coming out of the Register of Deeds office," Karen replied.

Wanting to get to the bottom of this obvious mix-up, Jillian walked straight back to the apartment where her aunt was making the beds and confronted her sternly but kindly, saying, "Aunt Carla, were you in Hot Springs yesterday?"

Carla spun around, looked at Jillian and began to fidget with the tags on the pillows.

"Why would I be in Hot Springs?" she asked, not making eye contact.

"I don't know, you tell me." Jillian hated it when people answered a question with another question.

"That's ridiculous, I went sight seeing yesterday, nothing more," she replied, "Why?"

"Karen's boyfriend Jon thought he saw you in Hot Springs yesterday," Jillian said to her aunt.

"Well it certainly wasn't me," Carla replied indignantly.

Eyeing her suspiciously; Jillian knew something was going on here because she obviously was lying through her teeth. Yet, rather than continuing the interrogation, she decided to drop it for now and headed back to the kitchen.

Aunt Carla, following Jillian through the dining room as casually as if nothing had happened said, "Victor and I are going into the art museum at Hill City today and then we may take a nice, leisurely ride up to Mystic and look around. Jake and Cindy are going over to Jewel Cave. Are you and Heath going with them?"

"I don't know. I haven't heard from him yet but I'm sure he will call me pretty soon. He knows that I had to get a couple of things squared away this morning before I could go anywhere," she said just as casually.

Though feeling suspicious of her, Jillian still tried to believe her aunt over the opinion of some guy she barely knew and most definitely didn't trust.

"You go have a great day," Jillian said, as upbeat as she could be. "Hopefully we'll be back here about six o'clock tonight for supper, and maybe we'll take in the Custer fireworks display this evening. How does that sound?"

"That sounds great! I love the sound of the Custer fireworks display ricocheting off of the canyon walls. It gives me goose bumps! Victor and I will be back early so I can help get things ready to go."

"Very good, now you two remember one teeny, tiny, little thing," she cautioned, "drive slowly and enjoy the scenery."

"Are you trying to tell me something, dear?"

Jillian laughed. "Now why would I do a thing like that? Just be careful, okay?"

"Okay, point taken, see you later."

Jillian tried to stay busy while she waited to hear from Heath. She thought he would have called by now. She had forgotten to get his number from anyone before they all left and now she couldn't get a hold of Carla or Jake. No reception.

Did he even tell me which motel he was staying at? she wondered. *Oh yeah, the Super 8, that's right. Maybe I'll call in a little bit; I don't want him to think I'm pestering him. Was he upset*

73

when he left last night? Did I do something wrong? I hate this.

With each passing minute Jillian felt her anxiety building, threatening to send her sense of reason careening over the edge. It was now after one o'clock in the afternoon and she had not yet heard from Heath.

"He's doing it to me again," she confided to Karen as she helps her with dishes. "I shouldn't have trusted him."

"He's doing what to you again, Jillian?" Karen questioned.

Forgetting that Karen didn't know everything, she quickly recanted her statement. "Never mind, it's not important. I have a stress headache right now. I'm going to take an aspirin and lay down for a few minutes until it goes away. Come get me if it picks up in here again, okay?"

"Okay boss, see you in about two minutes then," Karen teased. "We're fine right now, the steam table is refilled and we're ready for the next go round, so go lay down and I'll see you when your headache is gone."

Excusing herself from Karen and Roxie's pitiful looks, she retreated to her apartment. Taking off her apron and hair tie she shook her brunette locks loose from their confinement and looked critically at herself in the mirror. On the outside she was sure that she was nice enough looking, but knew deep in her heart that she has some serious trust issues to deal with. She had felt for a long time that the people she loved the most always seem to leave her—her father, her mother, grandpa and grandma and lastly Heath. She had struggled for years with what she understands to be a fear of abandonment and right now she felt paralyzed by it.

If I hadn't allowed myself to have feelings for Heath I would be fine, she thought. *I must stop this, he left me once and he'll do it again. The next time I see him I'm just going to tell him a relationship is out of the question.*

Lying down on her bed to thumb through a magazine, sleepiness took over her mind. Escaping these feelings that she didn't want to feel, she easily succumbed to its influence. Fear, mistrust and rejection, her mortal enemies, disappeared ever so briefly when she slept.

In what seems to her to be only minutes since dozing off, the phone rang. Groping around until she locates it on the nightstand, she answered sleepily, "Hello."

"Jillian, it's Heath. Sorry I didn't call you sooner but Kaitlyn got sick last night and I had to take her to the hospital." Sounding exhausted and worried, he continued, "She had her appendix removed this morning. I called as soon as I could get away."

"What? Where are you?" she asked as she sat up and tried to shake off the effects of sleep. "Is she okay?"

"She's going to be fine but she needs to stay in here overnight. We're at Regional Hospital in Rapid City, Jillian, I would sure appreciate your company if you're not too busy," he said in a voice sounding shaky and frightened.

"Of course I'll come. Is Ryan with you?" she asked him urgently, forgetting her earlier resolution to call this off.

"No, he's at the motel. Do you think Jake could pick him up and have him hang out at the lodge until Kaitlyn gets out of here? I haven't been able to get a hold of Jake. Do you know where he is, Cookie?"

"He took his family over to Jewel Cave; the cell phone reception is not very good over there. He should be back here any minute; I'll send him in to Hill City to get Ryan as soon as he pulls in! I'll get my things ready and come to town as soon as I can."

"I'll be watching for you, and Jillian, thanks, I appreciate your help."

"No problem," she replied.

Now fully awake, Jillian jumped out of the bed, grabbed a duffel bag and carelessly threw a few toiletries and clothes into it. Quickly brushing her teeth, she tried not to panic.

Kaitlyn should heal up fairly quickly, she reasoned. *It's a shame she's going to miss some of her vacation though. Oh, thank God, my headache went away.*

Jake and his family pulled into the lodge just as Jillian finished packing her pick-up. Jake approached her and her blue Ford Ranger pick-up and stopped.

"What's going on, Jillian?" he asked.

"Heath just called and said that Kaitlyn had an emergency appendectomy this morning. Ryan is stuck at the Super 8 in town and Heath was wondering if you would go get him and bring out here for the night? I think she is getting out tomorrow sometime. Would you mind?"

"Of course not, I'd be happy to go get him. Are you headed to Rapid City?"

"Heath asked if I would keep him company." She smiled. "Don't make a big deal out of this, Jake. We're just friends, got that?"

"I got it, sweetheart! Do you think everything will be okay with the restaurant?" He tended to be the one to worry the most. "What do you want us to do while you're gone?"

"Fortunately tomorrow is Sunday and we'll be closed," Jillian said, more to Cindy than to Jake. "At least that will be one less thing to worry about! Karen and Roxie are working by themselves; maybe you could help out with the trout pond, Jake. Cindy, could you help the girls if it gets busy again? You may have to cook, or wait tables, or do dishes or something like that; it's just been really busy the last couple of days."

"We noticed! We'll do whatever needs to be done and everything will be fine. Jillian, you just go, Heath and Kaitlyn need you," Cindy promised.

"Thanks Cindy, I owe you one," Jillian replied as she hastily headed toward Rapid City.

Chapter 12
Up to No Good

Driving back toward the lodge that afternoon, Victor and Carla Jordan discussed their plans.

When Carla Jordan left the lodge that morning she had no intention of sight seeing. She was not here as a tourist this time, she had business to attend to and nobody but nobody was going to get in her way.

There was money missing from her parent's estate and she fully intended to find it this time. For years she has been following a paper trail to no avail, certain all of the money from the uranium claims was not accounted for. Though she was determined to figure out what Bert had done with her mother's money she still couldn't help but feel a little guilty for deceiving her niece.

"There was no way my mother could have spent all of the uranium money on that snake Bert. He must have stolen it from her and hid it before he killed her. He probably figured he would bide his time in prison and recover it when he got out. Bet he didn't count on dying in prison," Carla reasoned again as she drove her husband back toward the lodge.

"I should have gotten more money from this estate than I did," she said for the thousandth time, though Victor never tired of hearing her say it.

"Your mother didn't have any business selling that campground you know. We should have gone to court and stopped it," he reassured her once again, justifying her feelings.

"And done what, Victor? She gave us the money and we spent it. We should have told her to keep her damn money and then taken her to court," Carla recanted sarcastically.

"Yes dear, she gave us the money all right, but only about half of what it was actually worth. Why she'd go and sell that property for so cheap is beyond me," Victor drawled.

"Why she sold it at all is what I've never been able to figure out. My father willed that property to me upon her death. Unfortunately, she was free to do whatever she wanted with it up to that point. Besides that Victor, the campground was only a small part of her and Ray's assets. This estate was much bigger than just the campground, there's cash unaccounted for and I intend to find it."

Carla knew that Victor shared her feelings concerning Bert and the lost fortune. They both agreed that Bert must have hidden the money on the Sleeping Abe. Carla knew the Crawfords had made millions of dollars mining uranium yet there was no possible way they could have invested it all in the resort. Even the money Lugenia spent on Bert's equipment and placer mining operation was just a fraction of the actual amount.

She was checking to see how many claims had actually been staked in Edgemont when that goofy looking boyfriend of Karen's had spotted her at the courthouse in Hot Springs.

"Too bad about running into that schmuck Jon Harden, he did come dangerously close to fowling up my plans," she laughed, thinking how she had covered her tracks so smoothly that Jillian took her side immediately.

She reasoned, "If the money isn't hidden in a bank somewhere, and I've pretty much checked them all, it must be stashed somewhere up near the old mill where Bert spent so much time hiding from my mother."

She and Victor needed to buy a shovel and a pickaxe so they could get up there and start looking. If they couldn't find the money this time she was going to try to get Ian to sell her the Sleeping Abe for pennies on the dollar. He didn't want it anyway. If she owned the property it would be none of Ian and Jillian's business what they did up there. They had headed into Rapid City to buy the supplies they needed to begin their search and were now heading back toward the Sleeping Abe.

She loathed the thought of going into the old mine shafts, as she knew they were highly unstable. By now it must be a primordial stew of stinky, molding mildew, but it was her only chance of finding what she so desperately longed for. Ray Crawford had seen to it that she had lived in high style, paying her rent and college expenses, but the money dried up when he died and her investments in the stock market had declined to the point of her needing to declare bankruptcy. She just wanted her lifestyle back.

She thought that the main tunnel under the elevator shaft should still be intact, as it would have been braced with the biggest timbers. Ian had confided in her that Bert had taken him down into it years before. Wouldn't it stand to reason that Bert had put the money in there somewhere? Bert was like a rat in a tunnel himself and that's where he would have left the money. When night came, she and Victor would investigate.

As Victor and Carla were leaving Rapid City with their wares, Jillian passed them on Highway 16 heading back toward the lodge. They did not see Jillian but Jillian got a full view of them.

"What are they doing in Rapid City?" she wondered out loud. "I'm just sure that was them."

Once again Victor and Carla were not anywhere near where they said they would be and she was now completely mistrustful of their motives. Right now she didn't have time to investigate. Heath needed her at the hospital and she was trying to get there as fast as she could without getting a speeding ticket.

She felt miserable for doubting him, for thinking he would leave her when he promised he would never do that to her again. Not knowing him well enough to trust him completely, she still found that her heart was taking her to a place she was all too familiar with—in love with Heath Connors.

He met her at the front door of the hospital. Together they sat in

Kaitlyn's room and watched his sick child doze in and out of sleep. Around 6:30 the doctor came in and assured them she was recuperating nicely and they should leave and let her sleep.

"She's in good hands," he assured Heath, "you, on the other hand, look like you could use some rest. Go get a motel, get some sleep and check back in here about eight o'clock tomorrow morning. I'll probably dismiss her around ten. She's fine, go get some sleep," he instructed.

Heath didn't have to be told twice, he was exhausted from being up with Kaitlyn the night before. Jillian called a motel nearby and made arrangements for them to stay. She realized that after this there was probably no going back, for her at least.

Heath and Jillian both knew they were entering unfamiliar territory sharing a motel room like this. They didn't speak as they unloaded their suitcases into the dark little room. There were two queen sized beds, just like she had asked for. They threw their luggage on the second bed and as soon as the door was shut their bodies came together, holding each other tightly.

When their wake up call came in at six-thirty they roused sleepily.

"Good morning, beautiful," Heath said as he brushed her hair away from her eyes.

Jillian wrapped her long legs around his as he caressed her once again. She succumbed to his loving touch as he gently kissed her tender lips. She loved him with all of her heart and all of her soul. She knew she always would and the thought scared her to death.

Arriving back at the lodge, Uncle Victor and Aunt Carla had found out from Cindy that Jillian was gone for the night. Carla felt empathy for Kaitlyn but nearly leapt for joy at the news that they had the freedom they needed to scout out the Sleeping Abe.

"Let's get up there while we have some daylight," she instructed her husband.

They drove Ian's old International pick-up Jillian still kept behind the old house. Carla lied to her son, saying she just wanted to look around for some pretty quartz to take home and they would be back in just a couple of hours. Jake, believing his mother's every word, helped her get the old, orange pick-up going. Surprised at how easily she could lie anymore, Carla promised herself that it would stop once she found the hidden treasure.

The road was still muddy from the downpour three nights ago, meaning that the mine would be a dripping, oozing mess. The old truck groaned out its protest as they climbed up the rough mining road to the Sleeping Abe. Victor pulled as close as he dared go to the entrance of the dilapidated old mill.

The wood of the old mill was aged a gray brown from years of weather, with most of the nails stuck half out of the boards. The whole formation was beginning to lean south away from the wind. Carla knew how this old mill had worked back in its hey day. Ray had explained it to her when she was younger.

They entered through the front door, half off of its hinges and let their eyes adjust to the dusty rays of sunlight streaming in through the cracks where boards had once been. It was silent except for the birds that had taken up residence in the upper chambers of the three-story structure.

In the past twenty years the head works above the main elevator shaft had collapsed and the pulleys and cables that had once lifted the ore cars out of the elevator had wedged into the deep dark hole. The railroad tracks and ties overhead that dumped ore from the cars into the tipple were rotten and broken as well. The tipple and the hopper that fed the ore to the stamp battery were leaning precariously and threatened to topple at any moment. Getting into the tunnel that ran off of the elevator shaft was going to be impossible. There had to be another way.

Walking back into the fresh air, they began investigating. Horizontal shafts had been cut directly into the side of the mountain and they knew there had to be an entrance to one close by. Carla began walking in one direction and Victor went the other direction, skirting the perimeter of the mill. Carla noticed an area where it appeared rock had fallen; she walked over to its base and discovered an entrance behind a pile of shifted granite, overgrown with grass.

"Come over here, Victor," she yelled. "You had better get the pick, some of these rocks are too big to move."

Stopping at the old pick-up, Victor grabbed the tools they had bought earlier.

"This tunnel should lead to the tunnel under the elevator shaft," he said as he began striking the granite.

Slowly the hard boulder began to break into smaller, movable pieces. Carla put on the gloves she had stuck in her pocket and began to pile them off to the side. By the time they had the entrance opened enough to enter it was too dark. They stashed the tools and headed back down to the lodge, leaving the exploration for another day.

Chapter 13
From the Mouth of Babes

Kaitlyn was dismissed on the morning of July 5. Heath propped her up in the backseat with pillows, and fastened her seatbelt. Kissing her lightly on the forehead he whispered, "Sorry you missed the fireworks display."

His love for his children was obvious to Jillian by the gentle way he handled his daughter. Jillian was just beginning to understand what kind of a man he actually was.

"Heath, you can't stay at the motel with a sick daughter, I still have the old house across the road. I could straighten it up and you and the kids can stay in there. It's a little run down but it's really cozy inside. Kaitlyn might feel more at ease out there with the rest of us, that way Cindy and I can help too." She waited for an answer.

"I don't want to be an imposition, Jillian, you still have to run the restaurant and you have a houseful as it is."

"Heath, I really wouldn't call you an imposition," she smiled sheepishly at him. "Maybe the boys would work the fishing shack; that would be worth more than gold to me right now. Besides, Ryan is a natural around the fish, he seems to love the sport. You must take him fishing a lot?"

"I have a little boat that we take out on the ocean occasionally."

Kaitlyn chimed in from the back seat, "A little boat! Daddy, our boat is not little. Jillian, he's lying, it's a great *big* boat, it has a kitchen, a *big* old fishing deck and we can even sleep on it."

She put a special emphasis on the word big.

"From the mouth of babes," Heath said shaking his head. "It's a small boat as far as some boats go." He grinned at her. "It probably wouldn't work on the puddles in this area though."

It occurred to Jillian that she knew many intimate details about the man sitting next to her but she didn't really know what he did for a living. He had been very evasive when she tried to get him to talk about it on their date to the amusement park.

"So Kaitlyn sweetie, tell me, what does your dad do for a living?" Jillian knew if she needed information Kaitlyn was going to be the source.

Heath laughed/ "You're a sly woman, Jillian Moore, and you don't play fair."

"Daddy invents things," she volunteered. "He invented a microchip that helps make a metal detector work better. Jake helped Daddy produce a whole bunch of microchips, 'cause he works in the Valley. Daddy has a company that makes metal detectors."

Jillian turned toward Heath, "So what are you, a rich CEO of some larger than life company or what?" She was astonished.

"Would you hate me if I was?" he asked her.

"Heck, I've always thought of you more as the beach bum type, not an inventor," she joked.

"But I'm a beach bum at heart, doesn't that count?" he smiled.

"Please Heath, move out to the house, I'm looking forward to getting to know all of you better," she winked at him so his daughter wouldn't notice the innuendo.

"What do you say, Kaitlyn, would you like that better than the motel?" he asked.

"I love it at the lodge, let's stay out there, Dad," she replied.

"You talked us into it then, Cookie. I'll stop by the motel and check us out."

"Excellent! I just hope the house isn't too primitive for your tastes, it is over one hundred years old and the floor sags in the middle, but at least it's clean."

"I'm sure it will be fine and I appreciate your offer so stop worrying, okay?"

"Okay."

Monday morning Jillian was up at 5:30 and by 6:30 the doors were open and her kitchen was humming with life. She mixed the dough for bread and let it rise next to the heat of the grill. Jake got up earliest and joined her for coffee.

"Good morning, Jillian," he greeted her, "what can I do to help you around here today?"

"You can just set here and visit with me," she replied. "Thanks for all of your help on Saturday; I really appreciate what you and Cindy do to help me here. It's crazy around the holiday but that's my biggest week-end, so I usually look forward to it. I'm sure you noticed that I'm a little distracted right now." She smiled, realizing how good it felt to just be happy for a change.

Taking an order from a family of five, she poured their drinks and went back to the kitchen to begin cooking breakfast for them.

"I understand you and Heath are in business together, Jake, what is it the two of you do anyway?" she asked.

"Heath is involved with a company from our area that mines. They needed an efficient way to detect metal in the earth, so Heath invented this metal detector that instantly analyzes the soil, breaks down its components and gives this company immediate feedback on whether there is sufficient minerals in the soil to make mining it worthwhile. He invented a microchip that has revolutionized the mining industry in Northern California. Because of it, these companies are able to go directly to the source of the mineral deposit and it is saving millions in land reclamation costs. All that I did was help him contact the right people to produce the chip. We aren't exactly in business together," he explained.

After delivering the food to her customers and refilling their drinks, Jillian went back into the kitchen to sit down and continue her visit with Jake.

"Why does Heath want to move out here if he has so much going for him in California?" she continued.

"I don't know what he has planned, Jillian, you know his marriage ended recently and I think he's kind of at a crossroads right now. I think they need a change is all," Jake replied. "Jillian, he wants you to be a part of that change; he has never stopped asking about you since he came out here with us in Eighty-five."

Jillian felt her face flush deeply. She had no idea he had given a thought to her after he left here and felt a stab of regret for the lost years between them.

Jake helped Jillian clear the table when her customers left. He went to work doing dishes and filling coffee cups as more people came in for breakfast.

Aunt Carla came bounding jovially through the door singing, "Good morning, good morning." She waved as she filled her coffee cup. She was wearing an old pair of jeans and had her hair tied up in a red scarf. To Jillian she looked stunning.

Jillian did not ask her about their trip into Rapid City two days ago. She only saw them in passing yesterday and she could tell they were off on some wild adventure again today.

"Victor and I are going to go up to the Sleeping Abe and look for rocks. Jillian, I have a rock garden at home and I need a nice variety of small rocks for it. I just love those shimmering, granite rocks that contain lots of mica. My friends are always amazed by mica; it's as common as dirt in these parts but not in Southern California."

"That sounds like fun, I'm closing a little early this week so if you get back and the restaurant is closed you'll know why," she warned her aunt. "Kaitlyn needs a little pampering; I want to help take care of her while she is recuperating. Instead of closing at eight, I'm closing at four."

"Are you sure you can afford to do that dear? Your winter nest egg isn't very big right now. Oh, excuse me, dear, that was uncalled for." She waved her hand in the air to dismiss her last statement. "You just take as much time as you need and everything will be just fine. Ta ta!" she said as she walked out the door.

Jake exclaimed, "I haven't seen my mother in such a good mood in…forever! She seems to be floating on top of the world."

The truth was she was deep underground, not on top of the world. She and Victor had been exploring the mining tunnels they had found on Saturday. They were up there most of yesterday and she felt confident that today was going to be the day she and Victor would uncover whatever it was that Bert had hidden.

There was a maze under there and it was going to take a little more time before they located the tunnel that was directly connected to the elevator shaft in the old mill.

They both suspected the money was in that particular tunnel but getting to it was proving to be more difficult than they had imagined because of cave-ins. She was not about to give up this easily; this money was her inheritance and she was going to find it.

"Damn that shyster Bert for ripping my mother off, though as idiotic as she was acting she had it coming to her."

"Now Carla, she's your mother, be nice," Victor reminded, handing her a pair of gloves.

"I know, I'm sorry, darling but she didn't exactly conduct herself in a very appropriate manner for being a well-to-do sixty-two-year-old, now did she?"

"No dear, she didn't, but we don't know the whole story either. She told us to butt out, remember? Besides, you're the same age as she was and here you are crawling around inside of dangerous tunnels looking for buried money. I think being a little, how do you say, eccentric, is genetic, honey."

"Very funny, Victor Jordan, now go!" she ordered, pointing toward the tunnel entrance.

Victor and Carla headed into the belly of St. Elmo armed with a shovel, two lanterns and a pickaxe.

Chapter 14
To Tell the Truth

Jake and Cindy worked alongside Jillian while Brian, Ryan and Greg waited on customers at the pond all day. They weed whipped, refilled the fish pellets, painted the little bridge that crossed the pond and fixed some of the poles that were broken. Jillian couldn't have been more delighted with them if she tried. Heath remained in the house with Kaitlyn.

The campground was full and their customers provided Jillian with customers. It was the seventh of July; even though the Fourth was over they were still unusually busy.

Jillian wanted to be across the road with Heath, not in the kitchen, but she stayed especially busy because Jake was doing chores for her that usually didn't get handled during tourist season. He replaced a fuse that insisted on giving her fits, he nailed in a downspout that had come loose, and he dusted the massive logs that made up the rafters of the dining room. He even vacuumed the elk's head above the rock fireplace. Before they knew it, it was four o'clock and she put the closed sign in the window.

When the restaurant closed, Jake and Cindy headed back to the apartment to take a well deserved nap. The boys asked them if they could take the van and go sightseeing.

"The only sights you guys want to see are of the teenaged female variety," Jake ribbed, "Ryan, you're driving; be careful, wear your seatbelts and watch for motorcycles."

Jillian slipped them each twenty dollars.

"Thanks guys, wish I could give you more."

Eagerly they took the cash and drove down the rode toward Hill City.

Jillian left Jake and Cindy in the apartment so they could enjoy some down time, or each other, whichever they chose. She walked down the drive, across the highway and softly knocked on the door of the old house.

Heath quietly answered the door.

"Kaitlyn's asleep, I was hoping you would come," he whispered. He took her hand and glided her toward the sofa.

"How's she doing today?" Jillian inquired.

"She was in quite a bit of pain. I gave her a pain pill about an hour ago so she should be out like a light." Still whispering, "You look like you've worked really hard today. Let me wait on you for a change, what would you like—iced tea or iced tea? I need to go to the store and get some supplies in here."

"Iced tea would be fine," Jillian replied. He went to the refrigerator to pour them tea.

"Maybe we can have Cindy set with Kaitlyn later and we can go do something really fun, like grocery shopping."

Heath handed Jillian the cool drink. "I walked over to the campground store and got a bag of ice," he said.

"I'll bet you paid a lot for it, they have the market on ice so they can charge whatever they want. You should've come over; I have an ice machine on the back porch. I would have given you ice."

"You were too busy today; I didn't want to bother you. How do you keep up with all of this, Jillian? I have been watching the amount of people who came in today, and I just don't understand how you can work so hard."

"What is my alternative, sweetheart? I have to pay bills in the winter with the money I make in the summer, besides I have five months that I pretty much do what ever I want. It's a good life, Heath; I can't see myself ever doing anything other than this."

Jillian decided that now was the time to pin him down She needed to know what he was planning and if it involved her she thought she had a right to know.

"You said you are moving here, what did you have in mind, moving to Rapid City or where?" she finally asked.

She could smell his cologne and it threatened to distract her from her primary purpose. She loved the smell of English Leather, though she was certain she herself reeked of grilled trout. Suddenly feeling self-conscience she scooted back from him a little just in case she did.

He scooted closer, "What's this, are you afraid of me?" he asked her.

"No, I need a shower, I must smell like a greasy old hamburger," she replied and it occurred to her that he had avoided her question by deliberately changing the subject.

"Delicious is how you smell, good enough to eat." He put his arm around her shoulders and pulled her close. He buried his face into her hair and softly nuzzled her neck.

"Jillian I know it's too soon but I'm crazy about you. I just want to be near you, I really don't have any other plans."

Jillian decided that the time had finally come to tell Heath the truth, that she had gotten pregnant the last time they were together. She told him about the miscarriage, the hospital stay and the intense sorrow she felt afterward. He sat, eyes wide open, taking in every word.

When she finished talking he buried his head into her shoulder and tearfully responded, "I am so sorry, I am so sorry. You didn't tell me, Jillian, it would have made all the difference in the world. I would have done the right thing by you if I had only known."

"I didn't want you to be with me because I was pregnant, I wanted you to be with me because you loved me." She mixed her tears with his. Years of sorrow and hurt began to melt as she finally confessed this torturous secret to him.

"I have never been happier in my whole life than when I was with you but I just didn't have the guts to stand up to my parents. I let them tell me what to do. Instead of following my heart I followed my father's pocket book. I would have loved to have had a life and a child with you."

Heath grieved openly for his lost child by putting his head in her lap and letting the tears flow freely down his cheeks.

"You wouldn't have these great children if things had gone differently for us, Heath. Sometimes things just aren't meant to be. It's okay, we're okay." She tenderly stroked his hair until they both felt comforted.

Sitting up, he kissed her softly. "I will make up for all of the hurt I have caused you, Jillian. I promise you that."

Unexpectedly, Kaitlyn began stirring in the back room. The conversation quickly switched gears to accommodate the child.

"How would you feel about going into Hill City with me to get some grub for this place? I just want to be with you and spend time in your company."

"I need to clean up," Jillian replied. "Give me forty minutes. I'll go ask Cindy if she will watch Kaitlyn and I'll call over here and let you know what she says. Try not to miss me too much while I'm gone," she said as she stepped out the door.

She felt lighter, as if this secret had lost its power over her and she was excited over the possibility of a committed relationship between them. She just hoped they weren't moving too fast.

Cindy said she would be happy to keep Kaitlyn and Ryan over at the apartment so Heath drove her over, dropped her with Cindy and picked up Jillian. They promised they would only be two hours. Jillian wondered why her aunt wasn't back from the Sleeping Abe but quickly decided it wasn't her problem. Though she was acting so suspiciously, Jillian couldn't help but wonder what she up to.

Chapter 15
Into Hell They Go

Carla and Victor had lost all track of time inside the shaft and when they emerged it was getting dark.

"Victor, we need to get back, someone is going to come looking for us, if they haven't all ready."

The tunnels inside of St. Elmo were numerous. They must have followed twenty different drifts. Several had caved in and she suspected the portico to the tunnel under the elevator shaft was one of them.

"We need to make a different plan," she schemed. "We're going to have to clear some of the debris out of that elevator shaft so we can go in directly from there. I know it's dangerous but if we're careful we'll be okay. Don't you think we'll be okay, Victor?"

"I don't know, Carla. It isn't my first choice but we'll give it a go and see what happens."

It appeared to them there was no other way into that particular tunnel except down that dangerous portal. She was willing to risk it. Even though she was sixty-two she could still climb down a ladder.

The problem was how to get a ladder up to the Sleeping Abe without anyone seeing them. They would buy a ladder in Custer and take it up there at night. That was the plan for tomorrow, but Carla knew she had not spent any time with her niece and she needed her to not be suspicious. She decided that tomorrow she would help her wait tables and cook in the morning and tell her she wanted to visit some of the rock shops near Custer in the afternoon. Jillian probably wouldn't notice anyway, she thought, she's too wrapped up in Heath right now to notice her.

On their way into Hill City, Jillian and Heath passed the three boys as they were coming back to the lodge.

"Let's take the boys up to the Sleeping Abe tomorrow, Jillian. I haven't been up there since I got here and I'm sure Ryan would like to see it," he suggested.

"Why don't you and Jake take the boys up in the morning? I'll call Ian tonight and let him know. Pan some gold on that contraption of Bert's if you want. I'm sure Ian won't mind."

"You don't want to go?" he asked.

"Except for you, Heath, that place has nothing but bad memories for me and I'd just as soon stay away."

"We'll call Ian together, I haven't gotten to visit with him for a really long time," Heath said. "Besides, if I'm going to sweep his sister off of her feet I would like him to know about it."

"You are hopeless," she laughed. "Did I mention that my aunt asked me what Ian is going to do with that property? She informed me that she wants to buy it from him, what do think is up with that?

"I have no idea; let's find out what your brother thinks of it."

Heath dialed Ian. Jillian was surprised he had taken the initiative and even more surprised that he had Ian's phone number already programmed into his cell phone. It seemed she couldn't get away from men who liked geology and here Heath was involved with mining himself. She believed that he was probably as well versed on the subject as Ian and her grandfather, but wondered about the possible connection with her brother.

"Here's your sister now, Ian, I'll let you talk to her for awhile. Hey, I'm looking forward to seeing you again. Uh-huh, yep, you too, bye," he handed the phone to Jillian so he could concentrate on driving.

"Hello Ian," it was Jillian's turn. "What have you been up too?"

Ian said it was fine with him if they wanted to go up to the Sleeping

Abe, just be careful he warned as he would incur the liability if anyone was hurt up there. Jillian assured him that Jake and Heath would watch the boys carefully.

"Hey sis," he said, "sounds like something is getting hot up in the Black Hills and this time it isn't a forest fire!" he said laughing in the phone.

"Ian, you behave," she warned. "On a more serious note, big brother, Aunt Carla asked me to ask you what you have planned for the Sleeping Abe, because if you don't want it anymore she would like to talk to you about buying it."

"What's that all about? Is she moving back to the Hills or something?" he asked.

Jillian replied, "No, I don't think so, but she's been acting strange lately, so anything is possible."

"Tell her I'm not really interested in selling, but if she wants to discuss it with me I would love to visit with her about it. I'm sorry I'm missing all the fun right now! Take care Jillian and let me know when you're getting married, okay?"

"Not likely! I'll talk to you later, you overgrown brat, take care of yourself. I love you too, bye." She pressed the red button. "So, have you and my brother been talking about anything interesting lately?" she inquired curiously.

"Nothing that you need to know about, Cookie," Heath said, grinning at her. "Where would you like to shop?"

At 6:30 the next morning Aunt Carla was up, showered and in the kitchen.

"Reporting for duty," she announced to Jillian.

"Are you done finding rocks?" Jillian asked her.

"Not exactly, I'm going to snoop around Custer this afternoon and see if I can find anything interesting, but right now I am here to help you out and earn my keep."

Aunt Carla made coffee, waited on customers, and did dishes, humming and singing to herself until Jillian was about to pull her hair out. She was happy her aunt was so jolly but it seemed contrived. Something had changed about her. Jillian didn't know what had changed but she was definitely behaving differently. She made a mental note to visit with Jake about it.

The men had taken the old pick-up and gone up the road around seven o'clock that morning and she figured they would be gone until hunger got the better of them. She had made baked pork chops with dressing for the special and if they didn't like that they could have a sandwich.

Sure enough, at twelve–thirty they all pulled into the lodge, starving from a morning panning gold from the shaker box, muddy and wet but bubbling with excitement. They each had a couple of small gold nuggets to show off and a handful of small, red garnets, January's gemstone. Often time garnets and gold were found together in the mortar box.

Jillian remembered Grandpa Ray telling her that garnets were once used to protect travelers from accidents far from home.

"Did anyone get bit up there?" she teased. "I hear there is a bug up there that causes gold fever. Did anyone get bit by it?"

"I did!" shouted Ryan. "That was a lot of fun and there's some really creepy stuff up there. Me and Greg found an entrance to an old mine but we didn't go in it, Jillian. We knew you wouldn't like it if we did."

"You found an entrance? I'm not too surprised; there are tunnels all over up there. I appreciate that you didn't try to walk into the one you found though, because that tunnel was dug out over one hundred years ago and could easily cave in. So, what does everyone want to eat?

She took their orders and dished up their food. They ate in the dining room so they could sit together and visit as everyone was in a jovial mood.

This is just too perfect, she thought as she watched them enjoying each other's company.

Heath caught her eye and motioned for her to go into the kitchen. Indiscreetly she went through the doors and a minute later Heath was behind her.

He put his arms around her waist and turned her around, "I missed you every second I was gone," he said and kissed her passionately. "The Sleeping Abe reminds me of you."

She had missed him too. He was all she could seem to think about these days, and she was flattered that he was thinking of her while he was up there.

"I saw that area of quartz where we met all those years ago," he whispered longingly, kissing her lips, her face, and her jaw line. "I remembered everything about it, how young we were, how soft your skin felt and your eyes glistened in the moonlight. I remember the wine we shared and the sweet aftertaste on your lips...."

"Hold on a minute!" she laughed as she wiggled out of his grasp. "You're practically undressing me right here in front of God and everybody! I'm glad you remember, but darling, someone is going to come in here and catch us groping at each other," she exclaimed. "I don't think your kids are ready to see that yet."

"I think you are mistaken, they love you as much as I do!" And with that, he made an exaggerated motion of covering his heart with one hand and blowing her a kiss with the other as he did a Chasse side step and waltzed out the door.

She chuckled to herself for a long time.

He's funny, she thought as she realized she had not laughed nor been this happy in her entire life. She was already dreading his return to California.

Heath didn't leave the lodge the rest of that afternoon, but Aunt Carla did, as did Uncle Victor, making a lame excuse about the rock selection being better in Custer and they would be late so don't wait up for them. Off they went in the old pick-up. Jake had given it a tune up yesterday, one of the many jobs he had accomplished, and it seemed to be running better than it had in years.

Heath helped Jillian finish up; he wanted her out of there and all to himself. At 4:00 she put the closed sign in the window and they sat down on the porch with a cold beer. Jake and Cindy joined them, the kids sacked out in front of the TV in the apartment.

Jillian began the conversation as tactfully as possible

"Jake, you haven't noticed anything unusual about your parent's behavior lately, have you?

"Well, they certainly are gadabouts," he replied.

They were all in agreement about that.

"Actually, Jillian, she mentioned something about Bert stealing money from Grandma, she seems to be preoccupied with the idea that there is more money somewhere, but she doesn't know where it is," Jake explained.

Jillian added, "I remember her saying that twenty-five years ago in the lawyer's office when they reread the will. I didn't understand what she meant at the time. Where would money have come from? Wasn't it all accounted for when the estate was settled?" She was puzzled.

"I have absolutely no idea," Jake said. "Mom seems to think there is money somewhere. She is an accountant, you know, and she would probably know if there was money missing."

Jillian continued, "But Jake, Karen's boyfriend Jon saw her in Hot Springs last week when she said she was going to Rapid City. I saw her and your dad coming back from Rapid City a couple of days ago when she had specifically said they were going for a drive up toward Mystic. The road to Mystic does not lead to Rapid City, so somewhere along the way they changed their plans or she just lied to me."

Jillian tried to remain calm but she could feel her ire building at the thought of Carla's deception.

"Well, it seems she is up to something and my dad is supporting her one hundred percent. They're thick as thieves they are. I'll try to figure it out, Jillian," Jake promised.

After finishing their beer, Heath asked Jillian to come over to the house with him for a minute. Jake and Cindy gave them a knowing grin as they strolled down the road, hand in hand. Once inside the old house Heath guided Jillian into her old bedroom and lay beside her on the double wrought iron bed Grandma had painted white for her so long ago. He stroked her hair, kissed her face, her nose, the downy hairs running down the sides of her neck. Yet, just as suddenly as he had begun to touch her, he stopped and rolled over.

"Not here," he said. "I want to take you to our special place with the beautiful rose quartz. I'm willing to wait for you Jillian, are you willing to wait for me?" he asked her very seriously.

"I've been waiting for you for twenty years, my love, I would wait for you forever," she confessed as she stroked the blond hair on his chest.

Heath rolled over and gazing into her eyes, he said, "I love you, Jillian."

"I love you too, Heath," she replied.

Carla and Victor stopped at the Ace Hardware store in Custer and bought the tallest ladder they could find. They slid it into the bed of the pick-up and tied a red scarf on the end that hung over the tailgate. Around 8:30 that evening they headed out of Custer toward Sylvan Lake, up and over the mountain they went, past the beautiful spires of granite.

Coming in on the east side assured more privacy for them. No one would see them turning at the old mining road that scales the east side of St. Elmo. No one would see them taking the ladder up to the Sleeping Abe gold mine.

Victor aimed the lights of the pick-up into the area that housed the elevator shaft. The shaft with the main head works caved in filled with debris from the collapse of the pulley system that once had lifted ore cars out of the tunnel below.

The potent stench of decay, the rotten timbers and mud oozing with insects did not deter Carla Jordan from finding the money she so desperately needed. She had lost her life's saving investing in high-risk stocks and she had nothing left, and nothing to loose at this point. She was broke, flat broke. Her husband did not even know how much she had wagered and lost.

They lifted the ladder out of the bed of the truck, carried it into the darkness and carefully, carefully lowered it into the depths of hell itself. They could not see down into the black abyss. They rearranged the ladder several times before it came to rest on something solid, possibly the ledge of a timber.

Victor tied a rope around his waist and secured it to the leg of the hopper bin. "It seems sturdy enough to hold my weight," he reasoned erroneously to his bride of almost fifty years. Gingerly, he started down the ladder, and to his surprise it was holding. He continued descending until his foot came to rest on the ledge that was supporting the ladder.

"Carla," he yelled up the shaft to his wife, to the woman he was risking his life for, "we need to do this tomorrow, there is just too much debris in here and I can't see, even with the lantern it's too dark. I'm coming up!"

"Damn it," Carla muttered. "We'll leave the ladder right where it is, no one will find it; we'll be okay until tomorrow."

Victor began a slow assent, taking one rung of the ladder at a time. Then something let out a low groan, the mountain herself perhaps belching her protest of trespassers, a creaking sound, louder and louder until all of hell's fury broke loose.

The timber under the ladder shifted and gave way, sending Victor careening to the end of the rope. He hung precariously, with the weight of his body tightening the rope, like a noose around his neck, it squeezed his ribs and cut into his underarms. He tried not to move but panic was pounding through his brain. For a few seconds he thought he was safe, he thought he had defied the odds, and then he heard the sound.

Weak from the effects of age and gravity, the hopper bin strained to hold him up. They heard the sound of metal twisting, breaking, but not being able to see the direction it was toppling from was terrifying and they both began to scream as it came careening down on top of them. The ancient dust settled over their bodies as blackness engulfed them.

Everyone was asleep at St. Elmo's Silverbell Lodge. No one had waited up for them; they had said they were going to be late.

Jillian woke up to Jake shaking her shoulder.

"Jillian, Mom and Dad aren't here yet, something is wrong, get up, please get up," he pleaded.

"What? What time is it?" she asked him, trying desperately to shake off the effects of a deep sleep.

"It's four o'clock in the morning and my parents aren't here," he said alarmingly.

Jillian sat up as sheer terror seized her, adrenalin pumping through her body. She sensed danger immediately, just as Jake had. She put on her robe and slippers and they headed into the kitchen. Jillian flipped on the lights and turned to Jake.

"My God Jake, where do you think they are?"

"I don't know,' he said. "You don't think they got in a car accident or something."

"Don't panic, Jake, we need to call the local authorities. Is there a nine-one-one service out here?" Cindy asked Jillian.

"Yes," Jillian answered as Cindy picked up the phone and dialed the number.

After taking down the information the dispatcher promised to send an officer out immediately. Cindy asked if there had been any car accidents reported that fit the couple's description. There had not been but for some reason knowing they had been in a car wreck seemed preferable to not knowing their whereabouts all together.

Jillian dialed Heath's cell phone.

"Hello," he answered groggily.

Jillian explained the situation briefly and asked him to come over to the kitchen so he wouldn't wake up the boys sleeping in the apartment.

"I'm on my way," he told her and hung up the phone.

They waited another half-hour for a police officer to arrive. It was 4:45 when his patrol car finally pulled up in front of the lodge. They took this opportunity to get dressed, and prepare for whatever the day was going to bring.

By 5:30 a.m., Sheriff's Deputy Glen Randall had located the pick-up. They all knew instinctively where to look—the Sleeping Abe.

Officer Randall and Jake entered the mill and though they did not see their bodies right away they realized something had happened inside and it was too dangerous to investigate any further.

By 6:00 a.m. the fire and rescue team were pulling onto the old mining road leading up to the scene of the accident.

What unfolded before Jillian's eyes seemed like organized pandemonium: lights flashing on at least a dozen trucks, firemen, EMT's and paramedics making plans on the best way to enter the building. The place became blazoned with activity.

The family huddled in a large brown tent the Sheriff's Department. had erected for a command post. Fog from the recent rain shrouded the mill, making the rescue even that much more difficult. With the air calm and cold, plunging to 46 degrees in the night, Jillian shivered just thinking they had been exposed to the elements for who knows how many hours.

Officer Randall stayed with the family as much as possible. He was trying to find out the history of the property from them. He was the Incident Commander for the operation, in charge of coordinating the rescue attempt. He was apprehensive about sending men into this death trap that should have been destroyed decades ago, and he was trying to find out from the family what was in there.

Jillian and Jake had never been in the mill, so they really were not helping the situation. They called Ian, and by telephone, he explained the layout of the old mill. Ian said he would be there as quickly as he could get a flight.

The extrication of Carla Jordan was the easiest, as she was thrown clear of the worst of the debris field. Within the hour she was being transported by ambulance the thirty miles into Rapid City Regional.

Deputy Sheriff Walter Halley knew this family. His grandfather had done some work for Ray Crawford many years ago. As a child he had tagged along with his grandpa and had met Mr. and Mrs. Crawford. Grandpa had let him go into the gravity house on the side of the hill and he had never forgotten what fun that day was. Determined to help in anyway he could, Walter decided to take Jake and Cindy into the hospital to be with their mother and hopefully their father, if he was found alive.

Jillian and Heath stayed at the scene. Karen and Roseanne had come out to stay with the kids down at the lodge apartment after Jillian had called them in a panic.

Victor Jordan was still missing. Officers assumed he had plunged to the floor of the elevator shaft and they all suspected he was probably dead. Before his body could be removed the rescue crew needed to stabilize the area, and it took most of the morning to remove the twisted metal of the collapsed hopper bin just to gain access to the elevator shaft.

Now, timbers and debris from the collapsed pulley system were carefully being lifted out of the elevator shaft. It was so painstakingly slow, Jillian and Heath thought they would never gain access to Uncle Victor. Nothing could be allowed to let loose and fall in on the victim or on the firemen. As soon as this part of the operation could be completed, a Stokes basket would be lowered and paramedics from the Hill City Ambulance and the Pennington County Rescue squad would be lowered in to administer to him.

Chapter 16
The Rescue

At thirty-eight years old, Glen Randall had been a Pennington County Sheriff's Deputy for twelve years. In all of that time he had never encountered a situation as harrowing and dangerous as what was unfolding on this day. What terrified him even more was the fact that this was not the only old mine left standing in the Hills, but he had never, in his wildest imagination, suspected sane people would attempt to enter one of them.

He knew he had pages and pages of reports to write and it wasn't going to be fun. The investigation into this matter was going to be long and drawn out. *The thing is*, he thought, *the owner of the property doesn't even live in the damn state*. He reached into his pocket for a stick of gum and watched as his coordination efforts played out in the ongoing rescue attempt.

Wait a minute, wasn't there some kind of a scandal up here before? Didn't some crazy guy murder a woman somewhere around here? He was thinking, thinking he had heard or read about it somewhere. He would do some research on it when he got back into the station.

Paramedics Todd Delaware and Stacy Pennel were both worried when their pagers went off. Dispatch had called for a search and rescue in an old abandoned mine shaft. That was a new one for them. Any call like that sent shivers up your spine. They knew that EMT's had transported a 62-year-old white female and that a male was still trapped in a deep hole. Rescuing lost people was what they both did best, but this was above any assignment they had done before.

Unfortunately, it was now their turn to get dirty. They were going to have to go into that nasty hole in the ground and bring that man to the top. They had waited all day for the right moment while crews of firemen and rescue personnel had made the scene safe. At 7:00 that night it was finally deemed safe enough for them to go in and lower the basket.

In a well executed plan, it was decided that Todd and a fireman from the rescue crew would go down and see what they could do. Stacey would stay up top, start an IV and do his assessment after he came up. Her training would kick in automatically, ABC: airway, breathing, and circulation, in that order.

Todd Delaware hated enclosed spaces. Yet he laid his fear aside as he donned a harness and slid down the side of the black hole to rescue Victor Jordan.

He could see what looked to him like a dead body with a rope tied around his sternum lying on his back in the mud below. "Good God, he looks dead," Todd called up to the waiting audience. Making a mental checklist to ward off the creepiness, he tried to focus on the task at hand.

Check his airway, see if he is breathing and check circulation, he thought. He was certain his circulation was already severely compromised by the effects of shock and cold, as his color appeared ashen gray.

Fortunately, the floor of the shaft was muddy and soft.

"At least the mud would have broken his fall and probably every damn bone in his body," Todd mumbled as he continued down the damp, rotten smelling shaft. They surmised he would probably have internal injuries as well, possibly even bleeding. All of these scenarios were running through Todd's head as he reached his victim.

"He's breathing, people! I've got a heartbeat and he's alive, but just barely. We've got to get him out of here," Todd announced to the rescue squad above.

A cheer went out amongst the men who had put their own lives in extreme danger to rescue this "tourist guy from California." That was pretty much all they knew about him. Todd quickly and carefully placed a C-spine collar around his neck and looked for injuries on the body as help descended from above.

Together they slid this two hundred pound cowboy onto a backboard and secured him with spider straps, then lifted him into the basket. Next they secured the backboard to the basket with another set of straps and when Todd was certain his patient was not going anywhere but up he gave the order to raise the basket.

Todd wanted out of this sinister place as soon as he could. It smelled of death and decay and he never wanted to repeat a performance like this again.

After Victor was successfully raised Todd took his flashlight and shined it into the bowels of the connecting tunnel. It looked as if most of it had caved in.

"What the...heck is this?" he exclaimed.

He took a glove from the jump kit and reached down into the mud and extracted what looked to be a bone. *Probably a deer or something*, he thought, but decided to take it up just in case.

Officer Randall alerted the hospital that the victim was out and they expected to be off of the mountain and down to the landing sight in another 20 minutes. Earlier in the day, he had his men scout out the best possible place to land a rescue helicopter. They had chosen the grassy area Jillian used to find four leaf clovers on, directly in front of the lodge, as it was the only place in that entire canyon big enough to clear the rotor blades.

Todd joined Stacy and started an IV. The ambulance took off down the rough road toward the makeshift helipad. The patient was cold, hypothermic; Todd covered him in blankets and secured the belts on the gurney. As Stacy was monitoring him, Todd attempted to get his blood pressure. They worked together like a well-oiled machine.

As soon as the ground crew got word the victim was successfully rescued, Flight for Life took to the air from Rapid City and was on its way. They had been prepared since nine o'clock this morning; standing by, ready to go.

In perfect synchrony the helicopter popped over the top of the east canyon wall and began its decent toward the landing zone just as the ambulance reached the highway, and turned onto the horseshoe shaped road in front of the lodge.

Victor Jordan was quickly loaded into the blue Life Flight helicopter, and within a few short minutes its engine was screaming for take off as the blades came perilously close to the front porch of the building. A crowd had gathered in front of the campground, watching in amazement as this machine, this modern miracle, effortlessly ascended into the cool, damp air and disappeared into the moonless night.

Yet as soon as one exhausting task ended, another began. Officer Randall drove back up to the old mill to complete his investigation even though he was completely dog tired. He kept the crew up there for another couple of hours scouring the crime scene, attempting to leave no evidence undiscovered.

Todd Delaware had handed him a bone and he intended to find out what the bone was from. It looked to him to be a femur of a human but it could have been from an animal, he wasn't sure.

He sent two firemen back into the pit to dig around in the mud. He was morbidly curious to know whether this hole, that to him resembled the entrance into hell, was the harbinger of any ghoulish criminal evidence. Within ten minutes they answered his question by uncovering a skull and several other assorted pieces of what was once a human. The back of the skull appeared to have been bashed in.

"Heck of a deal," he said. "We've got ourselves a possible murder scene here. See how much of that skeleton you can find boys, we'll send it to forensics and see what they come up with."

Chapter 17
The Hospital Scene

The two new patients did not even ruffle the routine at Rapid City Regional Hospital. Jillian and Heath found Jake and Cindy in the waiting room. Jake literally bolted as soon as they walked into the expansive, window lined room, grabbing Jillian and sobbing uncontrollably into her shoulder. Cradling her cousin in her arms like he was a wounded child, Jillian sensed his profound grief and tried not to add her turmoil toward this tragedy to his.

"I didn't know, Jillian, you have to believe me. I didn't know what they were up to."

"I know that Jake, none of us did, please come sit down," she led him to the sofa and he took a seat.

Cindy grabbed his hand and Heath sat across from him leaning forward, comforting his old friend.

"We're all shocked, Jake, none of us saw this coming. What do you think they were doing down there?"

Jillian knew the answer but Jake needed to say it, to vocalize it and to make their speculations seem more real. She also needed to see if they were on the same page with the reasons behind this unbelievable stunt.

"My mom was looking for money down in the tunnel," he said, drying his eyes. "How desperate is she for money to go to these lengths to get it?"

A nurse from surgery called to the waiting room and requested they be shown the way to the ICU waiting room. The elder woman at the desk walked them through the hospital to another wing which led to a smaller, more private area where they could all be together and wait. The room was set up for sleeping, with numerous roomy couches, and pillows and blankets stashed in an open cupboard.

Cindy had been trying all day to contact her sister-in-law, Jennifer, who was in Florida with her husband and no one but Aunt Carla knew where. Finally, after countless attempts Cindy contacted Tom's boss in San Diego and he gave her a number where Tom could be reached. Jennifer would be here tomorrow morning.

The stress of spending the day in utter panic was taking its toll on all of them and they found themselves sitting like puppets waiting for the puppet master to direct their next moves.

Dr. Lance Anderson poked his head around the door. No one realized he was the doctor until he introduced himself. He was in his early thirties, tall and handsome and best of all he was friendly and radiated a positive self-assurance that made them relax.

Sucking in his energy, he recharged their depleted batteries with his words of encouragement. He handed them food from a tray he had brought. They hadn't eaten in many hours and even though it was only peanuts and granola bars they ate robustly as he poured coffee and juice, waiting on them as if they were the patients. He quickly ascertained who was who in the family relationship so he could address them properly.

"We have your mother in the intensive care unit, Jake. I'm afraid she has sustained a rather serious head injury. We are watching her brain for signs of swelling, but so far none of that has happened. She does have a skull fracture above her right ear that is causing a great deal of concern, however," he began in a soft, soothing voice.

So soothing Jake did not at first realize what he had said.

"Is she awake?" he asked, not fully understanding the injury.

"No, she has not regained consciousness; she seems to be in a coma right now. We don't really want her awake anyway; her brain needs a few days to heal. We are monitoring her very closely and if we see a change in her blood pressure we will need to put a tube in to help relieve the pressure on the brain." He put his hand lightly on Jake's shoulder. "The next twenty-four hours are going to be very critical for her but right now she is holding her own and we are expecting her to recover fairly quickly."

Jillian felt as though she was just sitting there like a bump on a log. Not being able to think of a single question, she quickly discovered that she wasn't very good in crisis situations. She had had so many in her life that she had come to fear it. Her father's accident still burned in her brain like a hot flame. She felt panic that history was going to repeat itself. Grandpa and Grandma's deaths were equally shocking to her, making her feel powerless and out of control. She hated the feeling that something or someone was controlling the show besides her and she silently cursed God for making her endure catastrophes over and over.

On the other hand, Jillian noticed that Cindy was smooth as ice and felt gratitude that she knew instinctively what needed to be done, what questions needed asking, and who needed calling. She was neither harsh nor brash. She took the lead while the rest of them quietly sat back and let her take over.

"Doctor Anderson, can you tell us what is happening with her husband, we haven't heard anything yet, and we're worried about him," she asked.

"Mr. Jordan is in surgery right now, I am sure you will hear from them before long. He has some injuries to his abdomen, possibly a few broken ribs and he was bleeding from somewhere internally. I believe they suspected his liver might be involved."

"What are the implications of an injury like that?" Cindy inquired, the question never having crossed Jillian's mind.

"They may have to remove a section of the liver if they cannot repair it. Though that is a very serious injury, he has a good prognosis if that is all that is wrong. They need to look around to make sure nothing more was injured. We should know something in a couple of hours." He stood up, "Any more questions?"

They had a thousand but they sat back and nodded no.

The room once more became quiet and any energy remaining in the group went out the door with the young doctor. Heath motioned Jillian to a couch, secured a pillow from the closet and laid her down.

"Rest," he ordered. "I am going to check on Ian, I'll be back in a few minutes."

Cindy repeated the act of kindness to her husband, insisting he sleep. She rested in a chair sitting next to him, and lovingly stroked his hair until he was sleeping.

Jillian watched her, thinking that this was really what love was all about, sticking with your partner no matter how difficult or trying life becomes. She realized her uncle was willing to do anything, even put his life at risk to make the woman he loved happy. Even if it was the wrong thing, he did it for her because he loved her. She knew she had crossed that line with Heath Connors.

At 10:30 p.m., Heath walked in the door of the waiting room with Ian. Jillian breathed a sigh of relief at his presence. Except for Jennifer, the adults were all here, bonded together in the face of a horrible tragedy. Huddling together they made plans on how best to handle this situation.

Ian needed to see the Sleeping Abe, see for himself what had actually happened.

"I've needed help with the land reclamation for years but obviously no money is available from the federal government to help me and I don't have many options here," he insisted. "So sis, what are you going to do about your business tomorrow, are you going to be open?" he asked her, knowing full well that closing was going to hurt her ability to maintain through the winter.

"I really haven't given it much thought. I think I had better close up for a few days," she answered.

"What about deliveries and the food in the coolers? No Jillian, you have to carry on," he insisted. "Heath and I will help you tomorrow; we'll come back to the hospital when we are finished. Jennifer will be here tomorrow, Jake and Cindy will have Jennifer, and they don't need us hanging around all day."

"Thanks Ian, I would really appreciate the help."

Finally emerging from surgery, Uncle Victor was settled into the ICU unit. They were allowed to visit for ten minutes. Covering his mouth to stifle a guttural moan escaping from the depths of his throat, Jake nearly collapsed at the extent of his parents' injuries. He took in the scene at hand: tubes running from their bodies to containers, respirators, catheters, heart monitors, bandages, the sound of beeping; beeping making his head reel with the realization that they would be in the hospital for a long time and would probably need long term nursing care when they were released.

Life for them, from this moment on, was forever altered.

Chapter 18
Ian Comes Home

The first days after the accident were difficult. Sadness hung in the air as disbelief, confusion and guilt settled over them.

Ian and Heath tried to understand the whole assorted history of this place and looked for clues to solve the mystery of the so-called "missing money," though they both doubted it existed at all.

Though Aunt Carla was paying dearly for her greed they did suspect there was more to this picture than any of them had taken the time to look at or consider. Beginning to realize she may have had knowledge of something or someone that the rest of them were clueless about, Ian decided he was going to find out what had driven his normally sane, number crunching, kind and considerate aunt to the brink of insanity.

"Heath, we're going to the Sleeping Abe, hop in," Ian insisted.

Parking next to the scene of the accident, they carefully walked around inspecting the efforts of the men who had worked so hard to save his aunt and uncle. Yellow tape encircled the building saying "Police Line Do Not Cross."

There was an eerie quietness with only the sound of the pine trees seeming to whisper to each other about another tale of tragedy.

"If only these trees could talk, we'd have the whole story," Ian said breaking the silence.

"Creepy thought," Heath replied. "You know this place is

beginning to feel haunted in a historic kind of way. Even in the beginning, the Sleeping Abe had difficulty because its owners couldn't get along, from what I've read on the history of this old place that was the reason they quit mining."

"That would explain why the place is the way it is. They just walked away and left the tunnels all open. Usually the entrances were closed up with a stick of dynamite.

Walking in different directions they searched for clues. Heath came across the tunnel entrance first.

"Ian, come up here," he yelled.

Ian quickly made his way toward Heath.

"Look," he pointed at the entrance. "Tools, my god, did those two actually go in there?"

They stood in disbelief. "I would say they did, Heath. I think this entrance needs a stick of dynamite to close it for good."

They picked up the shovel and pickaxe that were resting at the entrance and loaded them into the bed of the pickup.

Next they walked over to inspect the placer mining equipment; the old machine, unbelievably, was still in good shape.

"This thing works like a charm, Ian," Heath said. "We fired it up and the shaker box worked and the engine sounded good. We changed the oil and added some fresh gas and it took off. We had a blast with it the other day. The kids loved it!"

"I'm glad to hear that, it's been almost two years since I messed around with it last. You know, Heath, I was thinking," Ian began chewing on a blade of grass, "Jillian always thought Bert was up to something up here. She always suspected that this mining equipment was a disguise he was hiding behind. When he was convicted it was because investigators found one old jar of mercury up here with his prints on the jar. They used money as his motive but when it was all said and done, there really wasn't any money to speak of."

"Just say for argument sake that there was some money up here, Ian, and he did know about it. Either he would have been up here looking for it or he would have buried it himself, right?"

"Right, if there was money. Bert was digging holes for some

reason. I always thought it was because he was putting the dirt through the shaker box looking for gold, but Jillian didn't think that was what he was up to."

"What did she think he was doing?"

"Jillian thought Bert was trying to kill me and make it look like an accident because he was looking for something up here and I was in the way."

Surveying the landscape, the two men, both educated in geology, began to notice a pattern of disturbances in the soil.

"Look up there, Heath; I would say old Bert started digging somewhere up there." Though the mound was grown over with new vegetation, it was still evident. They walked up to it and looked around.

"There's another one right beside it," Heath noticed.

With renewed eyesight they scoured the hillside for more evidence of digging, becoming aware of mounds of dirt pockmarking the whole area.

"Why would he dig holes and fill them in?" Ian asked, finally suspecting something other than mining was going on up here.

"He would have been looking for something, wouldn't he?" Heath remarked. "Seems to me old Bert might have been trying to find himself a buried treasure."

"Or, he could have been the one that did the burying and was trying to throw off any looky-lews, like me maybe," Ian replied, scooping up a handful of the black, mica-covered soil and letting it sift through his fingers. "Either way, I think my Aunt Carla must have thought Bert put whatever it is in that mining shaft under the mill. Why else would they have been in there? Probably not for exercise, that's for sure," Ian said.

They both chuckled. "That's exactly what Jake said the other night," Heath added, "Carla thought Bert had stolen a bunch of your grandma's money and buried it somewhere up here on the Sleeping Abe."

"You know, Heath, if a man had his hands on a pile of money, wouldn't it stand to reason that he would go out and spend it, not bury it? Why would he bury it on property that isn't even his? That just doesn't add up," Ian surmised.

Looking at each other they came to the same conclusion.

"Bert didn't have any money, he was looking for it, though," Ian continued.

"But Ian, if Bert didn't bury the money, who did? The only other people up here were your grandparents."

"I don't know," Ian said, shaking his head. "I think there might have been more to old Grandma Lugenia than meets the eye. We better get back, Jillian will be worrying and beside that I'm really hungry."

Jillian smiled with relief as she caught sight of her two favorite men coming down the mountainside. She had supper ready.

"Find anything interesting up there?" she asked as she noticed a serious air coming from Ian.

"Yeah, we did. Can we discuss it over chow, sis? I'm so hungry I could eat fish," he teased. "Just kidding."

Jillian knew full well Ian hated rainbow trout, always had, so she knew he was hungry. Sitting down at the table, Jillian began, "What did you find up there? Curiosity is getting the better of me."

Ian revealed his suspicions about Bert's activities but so much of it didn't make sense to him, he thought it sounded pretty implausible.

"Ian, remember when Grandma got so sick and was mumbling to me in the ambulance?"

"Oh yeah, I remember you saying that."

"'Find the pinkest rose, Jillian,' is what she kept saying. I didn't take her seriously. I thought she was just delusional, but now it seems as if maybe she wasn't. If Bert didn't bury the treasure then Grandma must have done it! Maybe it's in a pink box or something."

"It sounds as if Bert put those awful poisons in her to make her talk. Maybe he was trying to get her to tell him where the money was," Ian added.

"Could our sweet, dear grandmother have buried a treasure on the Sleeping Abe with the intent of hiding it from Bert?" Jillian asked Ian.

"That would make some sense towards Bert's behavior, Jillian, but why would she feel the need to hide money from him? She always had plenty of money and she always bought Bert everything he wanted," Ian replied as he scooped a mound of mashed potatoes onto his plate.

"Maybe he was threatening her over something, but there's no way of ever knowing the answer to that riddle," Jillian added.

"This Swiss steak is delicious." Heath smiled at her.

"Thanks," she replied.

Early the next morning, Heath, Jillian, Ryan, Kaitlyn and Ian left for Rapid City to visit.

Though Aunt Carla was semi-awake, she was confused and had no recollection whatsoever of any of the events of the day she was injured. Unfortunately, she had no recollection of any money, her motives, or even of her children. Jake and Cindy were devastated, but Dr. Anderson had assured them with time her memory should improve, though it may never be back to normal.

Uncle Victor was still in critical condition.

"Jake, you look like hell, buddy. What can we do to help out here?" Heath asked him.

Jillian's heart soared at the kindness in his words.

"There is nothing we can do right now but wait," he answered. "Thanks for asking though."

"I brought your suitcases. If you give us the key we can run them over to the motel for you on our way out of town, we'll just leave your key at the front desk with the clerk," Jillian told the Jordans.

Ian took Jake aside. "I need to talk to you, Jake. Would you like to run down to the parking lot with me and we can set in Heath's SUV?" he said.

"Sure Ian, let me tell Cindy," Jake replied.

In the parking lot Jake lit up a cigarette. "I quit you know, but the stress of this whole thing has gotten to me," he said.

"Hey, if you want to smoke, smoke, whatever gets you through the night, Jake," Ian replied. They smiled at each other and said simultaneously, "John Lennon."

Ian unlocked Heath's vehicle and when Jake finished his smoke they got in, started it and turned on the air conditioner.

"It's sure been hot this week," Ian commented, making small talk.

"What's up, Ian?" Jake asked.

"Hell Jake, I don't know where to begin with this story but if you have any input just chime right in at any time, okay?"

"Gotcha," Jake said as he sat and listened to Ian talk about the holes on the Sleeping Abe, the theory of Carla thinking Bert had Grandma's money, Jillian's suspicions that Grandma had hid the money from Bert and that Bert had probably been looking for it but never found it. Could Jake think of anything else they might need to fill in the puzzle?

"So what do you think?" Ian finally asked when he finished the explanation.

"Well, my mother thought someone had stashed money somewhere because it just didn't add up when her final accounts were settled. All of the money for the sale of the uranium claims in Edgemont was missing. Mom knew that, and I believe she has known it for a long time. I think the idea of that money sitting undiscovered somewhere just drove her crazy. She was having some serious financial difficulty because in February she asked if she could borrow three hundred bucks to help her make a car payment. Ian, she had enough money sunk in the stock market to make us all rich! But you and I know what happened to the stock market a few years back. I think desperation just drove her and my dad right over the edge."

"So you think it's possible that Grandma buried money on the Sleeping Abe too?" Ian asked.

"I think there is money somewhere. Maybe Grandma was hiding it from Bert, maybe Bert hid it from her, I don't know, but I trust my mother's instincts," Jake said sadly, knowing she would probably never have that kind of insight again considering the seriousness of her brain injury.

Lying in bed that night, Ian could not help but replay the past over and over in his mind. He wondered if Bert was trying to get him killed by taking him into the mine shafts. Now that he thought it through, he could recall Bert always standing out of harm's way.

Did he think I would interfere with his little digging project? Ian wondered. *He sure as heck wasn't going to inherit anything if I had gotten killed! I wonder what could have made Grandma feel the need to stash money. Maybe Bert did have something on her, but what? I am getting so bitten by the bug on the Sleeping Abe,* he thought, *I can see why this would drive a person crazy.*

Jillian too was awake in the quietness of her apartment. Just days ago it was full of people, the people she loved. Ian was sleeping in Jake and Cindy's bed and Heath was over at the old house with his kids. She imagined Heath's sweet lips on her. She wished with all of her being that he was in her bed as she missed him dearly. Just as they were beginning to rekindle their love toward each other this interruption came along, cooling the intensity of their relationship down. Though he had been wonderful through it all, supporting her and holding her during the rescue, she did not know how much more he would tolerate before giving up. She hoped that he was thinking about her too.

Chapter 19
The Proposal

Sunday morning, Jillian slept in late. At eight o'clock she awoke to an uncharacteristically quiet apartment. She wondered if Ian was in the kitchen.

"Ian, are you here?"

No answer.

He must be over having coffee with Heath, she thought and jumped into the shower then headed towards her kitchen. Ian had not made coffee and it appeared that nothing had been disturbed anywhere, not even a bowl for cereal.

Huh, that's kind of odd, she thought. She headed down to feed the fish and as she walked out the door she noticed that old house looked as if no one was there. The SUV was gone.

They must have gone to town for breakfast, she thought and continued toward the pond.

While waiting for their return, Jillian busied herself with cleaning. At noon she fixed a sandwich, turned on the TV and waited, yet no one came. She dialed Ian's cell phone but it kept taking her to his answering service. Becoming concerned, she walked down the road to the old house, looked in the front door and found that their bags were gone.

A mixture of panic, anger and indignation seized her as she headed back to the lodge. Locating her cell phone she dialed Ian's number.

Again, no answer. Then she tried Heath's number; same thing. Anxiety began working its magic on her.

"They must have gone into Rapid City but why wouldn't they have left a note or woken me up," she said out loud as she headed into the kitchen to see if there was a message on the table. Nothing was there.

He's gone, she decided. *He's left and he didn't even say goodbye this time.*

Suddenly, tunnel vision clouded her eyes and she realized she might faint. Sitting down on the porch chair she put her head between her legs to see if that would help. It didn't. Laying down flat on the cool concrete of the porch floor she became aware that her heart was beating very hard in her chest, and she could feel blood rushing through her ears.

Its two o'clock in the afternoon, where are they?

Driving into Hill City, she looked around for them but they were nowhere to be found.

Back at the lodge she lay on her couch and once again found herself staring into the cavern of the cold fireplace, unable to function. *This isn't happening again,* is all she could think. *Please, not again, I'm not strong enough for this.*

Later that night Ian gently shook her shoulder. "Sis, wake up, I'm home."

Fury pounded through her veins—at Heath for leaving, at her brother for making her worry. Jillian yelled without reservation, "Where have you been, Ian Moore!"

Taking a step backward, afraid she might take a swing at him, he replied apologetically, "Calm down, Jillian, I left you a note in the kitchen this morning, didn't you see it?"

"Do I look like I saw a note, Ian? I looked everywhere and there's no note in the kitchen or anywhere else. I have been sick with worry," Jillian wailed as sobs began to wrack her body. "Where is Heath? His stuff is gone, his kids are gone and no one bothered to tell me goodbye."

Her shoulders shook as hot tears of loss once again engulfed her. She covered her face with her hands to hide the shame she felt for being so vulnerable. Ian protectively put his arm around her.

"Let's go into the kitchen and find that note," he suggested.

"Did he leave me again, Ian, did he? I can't take it if he did; this is just too much," she cried out. "He said he loved me. How could he just leave? Everyone leaves me, what's wrong with me."

Ian began to laugh sympathetically at her uncharacteristic display of emotion.

"Heath didn't leave you, sweetie, he got a call late last night saying that his mom was sick so they left at four o'clock this morning to catch the six o'clock plane out of Rapid. Heath is coming back, but he's going to leave his kids with his ex-wife."

"How do you know? He told you but not me?" she asked, trying to understand this explanation.

"He called me. This whole Sleeping Abe thing has got my imagination working overtime and I was up early, sitting outside on the porch because I couldn't sleep. I guess he saw me outside and decided to call me. He's coming back just as soon as he can," Ian reassured her.

Ian looked around the kitchen and found the note under the steam table. "It must have gone flying when I closed the door," he said. "I'm really sorry."

"Where have you been all day?" Jillian asked, still feeling insecure about Heath but trying to regain her composure.

"I went to the courthouse in Hot Springs to see how many claims were registered to Grandma and Grandpa. The courthouse was closed but I sweettalked the cleaning lady into helping me. Aunt Carla is right, Jillian, there is money missing—about two million dollars, as near as I can figure."

"What! You're kidding, right?"

"I'm not! I've done a rough estimate of how much they paid for this place." He pulled a folded piece of paper out of his jeans pocket. "And I figured in my college tuition, and estimated how much she spent on that old shyster Bert." He sat the paper down in front of Jillian. "They sold two hundred claims, and they were sold for twenty thousand dollars each. Jillian, that's four million dollars!"

"I had no idea." Jillian was aghast. "They didn't live like they had that kind of money; they made us work our tails off when we were younger. We could have been living in the lap of luxury, Ian." They both laughed at the thought.

"They spent two hundred thousand buying this property, about a hundred thousand on Bert and fifty thousand on me. They bought antiques but that stuff was worth…seventy-five thousand at the most."

Jillian was beginning to see the logic in Ian's figures.

"So after taxes and stuff like that you figure there should be about two million dollars unaccounted for, is that right?" she asked him, realizing he was making sense.

"That's at the very least, Jillian. Aunt Carla knew about it too, she was suspicious from the beginning, but with Bert taking over Grandma's life like he did she probably didn't get the opportunity to ask where it was and you know Grandma wasn't easy to talk to about money," Ian surmised.

"Are you sure she only spent one hundred thousand on Bert?" Jillian asked.

"Positive," he replied.

"Why did she act like she spent so much money on Bert then? How did Bert find out there was money and where is it now?"

Ian chuckled. "That's what we need to find out, little sis. Only wish we knew how."

Ian had taken two weeks' vacation and one week had already flown by. Jake needed to get home, his time was up as well and they needed to make preparations for Carla to receive some extended nursing care. Jennifer and Cindy made the arrangements to fly her home and on the fifteenth of July, they took her to San Diego, California, and put her in a rehabilitation center. Jennifer stayed behind with her dad and Ian and Jillian took turns looking in on him.

Though Uncle Victor was improving physically, his infection was gone and his liver was healing, he still was not waking up like the doctors thought that he should. He had been given a CT scan to see if something was wrong but they came up with nothing. According to Jennifer he was to stay one more week and if his mental clarity did not improve he would go to the same center as his wife.

Jillian has not heard a word from Heath and she was a nervous wreck. Twice she cried on Karen's shoulder and twice Karen convinced her, though temporarily, that everything would work itself out.

Karen was still hanging around with that strange little man Jon Harden, hitching rides to work with him every day. Jillian thought that for a logger he didn't seem very motivated.

"He's a strange little dude, Ian," Jillian confided in her brother. "Snoopy, too I don't like him."

Finally, on Friday, July 17, as Jillian was trying unsuccessfully to get to sleep, she heard the sound of tires slowly pulling into the driveway, disturbing the gravel ever so slightly. She worried because Ian had transferred his stuff over to the old house so he could sleep in late. She sat up in bed as Heath opened the door and whispered her name. "Jillian, Jillian, are you here?"

"Heath, is that you?" she said as she reached for the light.

Before she had a chance to turn it on he was on top of her. He rolled her up on top of him, covers and all. She kissed him a thousand times before either one said a word.

"I missed you so much. My god woman, what you do to me," he said as he rolled her onto her back, drinking in her essence. Leaving her had haunted him and he couldn't wait to reunite with the woman he loved.

The moonlight was illuminating her face and her beautiful eyes mesmerized him completely.

"My mom is such a drama queen, Jillian. I got back here as soon as I could. You'll have to get used to her, sweetheart, if she is going to be your mother-in-law."

"Oh really, my mother-in-law," she stammered as she sits up in bed.

Heath turned on the light as he slid to the floor beside the bed.

"Marry me, Jillian. I can't live without you for another minute. I love you and I want to spend my life with you," he proposed as he reached into the pocket of his jean jacket.

Holding up a ring for her to see, he took her hand. It was a simple ring with a slim gold band and a one-carat diamond shining brighter that the evening stars.

"What do you say? Please marry me, woman, my knee is going to sleep down here."

Jillian rolled her legs over the edge of the bed and slipped down beside him. She wrapped him in a sweet embrace and kissed his face.

"I would be honored to marry you. You are the only man I have ever loved." Tears of joy streamed down her face. "I haven't cried this much in my whole life," she said as Heath slipped the ring on her finger.

"How did you know my size?" she asked as she wipes at the tears.

"I asked Ian to measure your rings on the side of your bed before I left. He snuck into your room while you were snoozing away. He took a piece of string and wrapped it around that Black Hills gold ring you always wear."

"You mean Ian knew about this all along? You two are so sneaky, I didn't suspect a thing."

"He was my accomplice, couldn't have done it without him. He is going to be my best man too. I already asked him."

"You have a lot of confidence in yourself, Heath Connors," she laughed as she brushed his curly hair from his face.

Laughing the happiest laugh he can ever remember in his life, he kissed her as they rolled gently backward, onto the floor. Propping himself onto his elbow he whispered quietly into her ear, "We're waiting until we're married to be together again, Jillian. I have taken too many privileges with you already. I'm an honorable man, and I just want to do the right thing this time."

Heath became very serious. As he stood up, he took Jillian's hand and helped her to her feet.

"Now, love of my life, if you will excuse me, I will be bunking over at the old house with your brother. We can make wedding plans tomorrow."

Tenderly, he took her face into his hands, kissed her and promised, "You have to trust me, Jillian. I will not leave you, not ever. I know you don't exactly have confidence in me yet but I am going to spend the rest of my life loving you and taking care of you. Do you understand?"

"I understand," she replied as she kissed him one last time.

Chapter 20
Oh the Bones, Oh the Bones

Early the next morning Jillian was surprised to see Deputy Sheriff Glen Randall at her kitchen door.

"Come in, Officer Randall, what can I do for you?" Jillian asked as she offered him a cup of coffee. Politely she inquired, "How is your investigation going?"

"Well, Miss Moore, the night your aunt and uncle were injured a discovery was made by the paramedic who rescued your uncle," he began. "It seems there were human bones in the bottom of that elevator shaft. We have had them analyzed and they seem to belong to a male, approximately 70 years old. Forensics approximates the time of death to be 1979 or 1980. Were you ever aware of anyone fitting this description missing in this area?"

Jillian was stunned. "No, Officer Randall, I have absolutely no idea who it could have been."

"Please call me Glen," he insisted.

"Okay, Glen, I'm speechless on the subject. Let me get my brother over here."

She called Ian and woke him up. With his hair disheveled and looking as confused as she knew they both felt, he quickly arrived in the kitchen.

"Ian, this is Deputy Sheriff Glen Randall," Jillian said nervously as she introduced them. "He was the rescue coordinator the other night."

"Nice to meet you finally, Ian. You're the owner of the Sleeping Abe, are you not?"

"Yes sir, I'm the owner. I inherited the property when my grandmother died."

"What year did you take ownership of the property, Ian?"

"My grandmother died on Flag Day actually, June fourteenth, 1979, and I took ownership when her estate was settled in November of that same year. Why? Is there a problem?" He looked at Jillian and knew from her expression something had happened.

"The night your relatives were injured," Officer Randall continued, "a paramedic made a discovery in the mineshaft. He noticed a bone sticking out of the mud. We excavated the sight and found several other body parts, including a skull. The bones were sent to a forensics lab and the results came in last evening."

Ian was confused. "Who was it?"

"We were hoping you could help us answer that question. He's a male, approximately 70 years old and died around 1979 or 1980. That's about it, we don't know any more than that."

Ian again looked at Jillian. They are both frightened at this turn of events. "Everyone who has ever lived up here is accounted for. I can't even imagine who it would be."

"Wasn't your grandmother murdered here about that time?" the officer asked.

"Yes, her boyfriend Bert went to jail for that crime," Ian replied.

"Is it possible he could have also murdered this person? He would be our prime suspect at the moment."

"Anything is possible with that guy, he was trouble. We wouldn't put anything like that past him," Ian replied.

"I would like it if you could come into the hospital in Rapid and give a little blood donation. We'll need to rule out any family connection. They will do a DNA profile; it will probably take about a month to get the results back. We need to send them to the state crime lab and that takes awhile. If you plan to leave the state you need to contact me so I know where you will be."

"Am I a suspect?" Ian asked.

"Everyone is a suspect until we figure out who this person was. Just let us know where you're going to be so we can contact you later."

When Officer Randall got up to go Ian followed him outside and they talked for awhile out of the hearing range of Jillian. She thought that he seemed friendly enough, but the news he brought made the adrenaline pump through her body. She was as frightened as the night of the accident but she wasn't sure why. They didn't kill anyone, but they had obviously lived with a man very capable of it.

"Who was he? Who could it possibly be?" she wondered.

Ian and Heath decide to go back up to the Sleeping Abe property early Monday morning. It seemed they had their heads together quite a bit lately, but didn't let Jillian in on whatever it was they were arranging.

Yet later that morning, Jillian noticed two large trucks carrying two large caterpillar tractors turn off of the highway and head up the narrow, rocky little road toward the Sleeping Abe. Jillian wiped dough from her hands and headed out the door. She had to see this one for herself.

Jumping into her Ford Ranger, Jillian followed the parade up the side of St. Elmo. She pulled out of the way of the semi-trailers as they unloaded the big cats on the side of a bank. Ian and Heath were directing the bulldozer operators, as it was apparent they were going to raze the mill into a pile of rubble. A dump truck rumbled up the road behind her, poised in a position the front-end loader could easily access.

"Ian," she yelled, "do you think you should be doing this? It's a crime scene."

"Remember when I was visiting with Officer Randall yesterday? Well, I got permission from him to tear it down! The police have everything they need and they are happy it is coming down. I even have demolition papers. We're good to go girl, set back and watch the show."

Knowing this event was for posterity, Jillian quickly headed back to get her camera. The structure was well over one hundred years old and it deserved to be photographed, as the likes of it would never pass that way again. She felt its history was indelibly tied to her own past, as well as America's past. The last few remnants of gold fever in the Black Hills being lost forever was sad to think about, yet Jillian felt relief at the thought of it being gone.

"Karen, I'll be back in one hour, hold down the fort," she exclaimed excitedly as she got back into her pick-up and headed up the mountain.

Snapping pictures in black and white, she photographed the demolition, the clean up and the front-end loader filling in the elevator shaft, forever sealing off the only entrance to the tunnel below. She knew this would have to be done again when the rain settled the dirt deep into the tunnel. It may need to be done many times until it settled in for good. She was sad that it has been a grave for some unknown man for so many years, but she and Ian could not for the life of them figure out whose bones were so thoughtlessly left in the shaft.

When the rubble pile was finally cleaned up, the crew carefully and efficiently leveled the ground. She knew Mother Earth would heal herself with the passage of time.

"I've called a crew from Tech to come up and take some soil samples for me," Ian yelled over the rumble of the big machines. "We're going to see if any of that mercury is still hanging around in the soil. If it's still at toxic levels, the EPA is going to get a call."

"I'm so proud of you, Ian; I know how hard this has been for you."

"It's not that I didn't have the desire, Jillian, I just didn't have the money. Heath is paying for half of the demolition and I am paying for the other half. He said if we need a full-scale topsoil removal he would lobby on our behalf and try to get us the money. If not, he's paying for it out of his pocket. Can you believe that, Jillian?" Ian asked, tears brimming his eyes.

"Yes, Ian," Jillian said. "I can believe it."

Now that the mill was gone, Ian had decided to keep the shaker box that Bert had built right where it was. Jillian wasn't sure.

"Don't you think it's just a tad bit ugly? Maybe if you tied some ribbons around it and put some lipstick on it that would help," she joked.

"I'll make it so it isn't quite so unsightly, Jillian. This old contraption is still in good working order and with a little fixing up we could still use it. Sounds like the kids had a good time panning gold out of it. Do you suppose other people would enjoy it as well?"

Ian was excited, "You know, this kind of equipment is hard to come by these days. It's a piece of history. Besides that, I'm thinking of building a house up here. I really miss the Black Hills and I think I'm ready to come home. What do think about that, Jillian?" Ian had excitement in his eyes for the first time in years.

Jillian climbed and stood up on a granite rock, surveying the property and announced, "Ian, a house would be perfect right over there. It's above the mill just in case the water table is polluted." She jumped down and put her arm around her brother. "I think it's a wonderful idea, just wonderful."

Chapter 21
Wedding Plans

Heath and Jillian decide to have their wedding up where it had all begun for them, near the outcropping of rose quartz on the Sleeping Abe. The shape of the quartz vein was situated in such a way that it made a natural arch in the side of the hill. The spruce trees encircled the rocks to make a natural amphitheater. They both agreed that it was perfect.

They decided that the wedding should be August 21, after the Sturgis Bike Rally so there wouldn't be as much motorcycle traffic, congestion and noise.

Walking around the vicinity, Heath and Jillian happily made plans, such as the best place to position chairs for the ceremony. They agreed to keep the decorations simple, just enough to optimize the innate splendor of the area. They also agreed that balloons or crepe paper would be tacky; anything unnatural would cheapen its innate beauty.

They decided on an arch filled with pine boughs and dried flowers, set about three feet in front of the rocks. Pink roses and carnations would sit to either side in standing baskets. Pink and white mums would sit in pots at their base and a spray of white lilies would lie across the top of the rose quartz arch. Jillian would carry a bouquet of pink and white baby roses to remind her of her grandmother.

"It's going to be beautiful, because you're beautiful," Heath said.

Jillian knew Karen Sanderson would be her maid of honor and she would ask Karen's mother, Roseanne, to be listed as her guest of honor in place of her parents. She asked her to help serve the cake and to keep track of the gift table, to which Roseanne tearfully agreed.

The whole area needs to be swept of conifer needles and cleaned up. A few branches had fallen nearby. Ian and Heath would cut them up for firewood and take to the lodge to burn. The reception would be held in the dining room of the lodge, where they would hire a band and have a dance.

Jillian once had loved to dance. When she was younger she was glued to the Nutcracker Suite every Christmas. To this day she supported the arts as often as she could and swore someday when she won the lottery she would donate the proceeds to the struggling thespians at the Black Hills Playhouse in Custer State Park.

Some day, she thought.

Lost in thought, Jillian finally realized that Heath was standing on top of the quartz arch looking amusingly puzzled.

"What's the matter, sweetheart?" she asked.

"Jillian, look at that big piece of quartz over there."

She turns to where he is pointing, brushing the Sugar Plum Fairy from her thoughts. "I see it, it's really big and in the way, don't you think?" she replied.

"That's not it! Look at the way these rocks are sitting," he said as he stretched his arms in a panoramic motion. "They are in an outcropping or a vein, if you will. That rock really shouldn't be there. It should be sitting over here with the rest of the nice little quartz family."

He was being factious but completely serious. They each stepped closer to inspect it.

"Heath, it is absolutely the most beautiful pink quartz that I have ever seen," she exclaimed!

"I can tell you now, Jillian, that it's been moved to this spot. I'm fairly certain that rock did not originate here. Look here, it's sitting on top of the soil, not down in the soil like those over there," he said, pointing to the outcropping. "Unless you've had an earthquake lately or that rock grew legs, I would say that someone put it there on purpose."

Rolling her eyes at him she replied, "I love your simple terminology, darling, but didn't it just emerge out of the earth? You know, geological pressure, erosion baring it to the world, that kind of thing?"

"Not likely. Look around, there is no evidence of other quartz in this immediate vicinity and it's just too clean. I just find it unusual is all, from a geological standpoint of course."

"Of course," Jillian replied. "So, you don't feel it grew legs and walked over here then?" she teased him, wrapping her arms around his strong body.

"Not in my estimation, darling," he said as he gave her a quick kiss on her forehead.

"It is undeniably beautiful, Heath, but nonetheless, it is in the way. We need to get Ian to move it with the front-end loader," Jillian said adamantly. "Let's take it down to the lodge and set it on the grassy knoll where the clover grows. I can plant pink and white petunias around it next spring."

"Not a bad idea, Cookie, not a bad idea."

Back at the old house, Jillian and Heath found Ian on the phone with Shawn Weicher, Ian's old professor at the School of Mines and Geology in Rapid City. Shawn had been analyzing the soil samples taken the day before.

"Heath, Jillian, come in, I've got some good news! The mercury levels in the soil are within normal ranges for government standards! They are at the high end, but it looks like we're not going to need to tear up the streambed. Unfortunately, they feel that there is probably a low spot where some contaminates could have pooled. They feel there is probably still a hot spot, but not on my property. It would be the responsibility of the Forest Service to remove it if it is further downstream."

Ian continued, "Shawn is going to contact the office in Hill City and let the Forest Service know they need to investigate the matter more thoroughly."

"So, it's not on your property and your property is okay?" Heath asked excitedly.

"There will be money for reclamation if it's on Forest Service Land. Yee haw! That is some seriously good news!"

"We could use some good news around here," Ian said.

"That is the best of news, Ian, I'm so happy for you." Jillian hugged her brother. "Ian, wasn't it Bert who first started the rumor about contaminates being in the ground water?"

"He used to tell me my hair would fall out if I drank water from the stream."

"He was just trying to scare you so you would stay away is all. He was looking for buried treasure and didn't need you figuring out what he was up too."

"I know, little sister, but he scared the damn daylights out of me just the same," Ian confessed angrily. "What was Grandma doing with a jerk like that?"

"Trying to make people believe she spent wads of money on him, when in reality she didn't," Jillian replied. "Whose to say that maybe she killed the bones in the elevator shaft."

"I've already thought of that one, Jillian. If Grandma killed someone, maybe Bert was blackmailing her or something, though that theory doesn't make sense to me."

Heath exclaimed, "Hey, let's get out of here for a little bit. We have a job for you up on the Sleeping Abe, Ian."

"What's up?" Ian asks.

"We have this lovely little rock needing a new place to call home. It's not being invited to the wedding," Heath said, winking at his future bride.

"What does that mean? You need a rock moved or something?"

"Would you mind, Ian? It's in the way," Jillian asked.

"Anything for the bride-to-be," he replied as he grabbed a pair of work gloves off of the table. "Let's go," he announced.

Twenty minutes later they were standing in front of the mysterious stone. Ian backed up Heath's belief that it was in a peculiar place and agreed with Jillian that it was the most beautiful rose quartz he had ever seen on the property.

"What do you want to move it for? We could dress it up in a little tuxedo and call it an usher," Ian joked.

"Ian, for god sakes, move the damn rock!" Jillian yelled at him, and then cracked up laughing. "I swear I'm surrounded by a bunch of clowns."

"We'll keep your life interesting, won't we," Heath said, still laughing at Ian's joke.

"That's for sure," she replied.

Ian started up the front-end loader, and positioned it over the top of the massive rock. He dug down underneath and lifted. Something scraped, but it was not a sound of nature, more like a noise like metal hitting metal.

"What was that?" they asked simultaneously, looking at each other.

Ian finished loading the rock into the bucket of the loader then backed up and shut it off. Jumping out of the cab, he frantically checked to see what he had hit.

Jillian, realizing what had just happened, started jumping up and down as she screamed, "That's it, that's it! Grandma said the pinkest rose, Heath, oh my God, and there it is right in front of us! I didn't believe her but it makes perfect sense, she told me to find the pinkest rose, the pinkest rose quartz!"

Jillian, very close to hysteria, began to cry. Trying to stifle his own excitement in order to calm her down, Heath embraced her in an enormous bear hug and wiped her tears with the sleeve of his flannel shirt.

Ian was on his hands and knees, madly moving dirt away from what appeared to be an old steamer trunk, the elusive treasure perhaps, hidden from view for over twenty-five years.

Heath ran over to the old pick-up and got the shovel Uncle Victor had used in his failed attempt to find the missing money.

"We had better use a shovel, Ian, this thing looks to be pretty good sized."

Heath dugs cautiously around what appears to be a rusty, green railroad trunk. When the handles were showing sufficiently, they both grabbed a hold of them and with all of their might pulled it from its hiding place.

Breathlessly, Ian exclaimed, "Let's get this bad boy down to the lodge where we can open it, folks. It just might be Christmas in July!"

After hauling the trunk and the rose quartz down the hill in the front-end loader, Ian carefully unloaded the trunk on the front porch and then set the rock in its place of honor on the knoll. The rock looks spectacular, luminous, as if it possessed an inner light.

Ian parked the loader on the east end of the lodge, out of the way. Jillian made iced tea as she waited for her brother to finish his chore and join her. When Ian was done they congregated in front of the trunk. Whatever it contained had cost four people a lot of pain and suffering: Grandma, Bert, Victor and Carla. Jillian felt a little stab of fear, hoping they were not opening Pandora's Box and unleashing something horrible into the world.

As Karen, Roxie, Jillian and Heath watched, Ian carefully pried the rusted lock off the box. Slowly he opened the lid, heightening everyone's suspense to the point of wanting to hit him with a shoe. Simultaneously they gasped, not believing what they were seeing.

It was full to the very top. Their mouths were agape at the enormity of their find. First, Ian lifted an old burlap bag full of cash from the top of the trunk and then counted the neatly wrapped stacks of bills. They were in one hundred dollar denominations, neatly wrapped in stacks of fifty. They counted twenty piles of one hundred dollar bills in stacks of fifty and estimated the amount of cash to be about one hundred thousand dollars.

Sitting under the money was a mound of stock certificates wrapped in plastic and beneath that were forty dazzling bars of gold.

"No wonder this thing was so heavy," Ian remarked as he sat one of them on Jillian's bathroom scale.

The scale registered each bar at ten pounds, for a total of four hundred pounds of solid gold. The shock and awe of the onlookers grew as they ever so carefully removed the aging stock certificates from the plastic wrap.

"Jillian, I think we have a small fortune here. These stock certificates are mostly railroad, the Burlington Northern and the Union Pacific. Here are a few from the Homestake Gold Mine."

Ian's jaw dropped in awe as he looked at Heath and Jillian and naively asked, "What do we do next?"

"Call in the Royal Canadian Mounties and see if we can get Dudley Doright over here," she said, trying to lighten up the serious mood.

Ian slapped her on the knee with the stack of stock certificates. "Now who's the clown?" he said as he jumped up, grabbed Roxie and started dancing on the front porch, whooping and hollering.

"We're rich!" he shouted. "I know these railroad stocks are worth millions, the BN stock split when the railroad merged with the Santa Fe. Homestake Gold Mine closed up, so these stocks aren't worth anything, but who cares, right!"

"Take it easy, big brother, we need to think about this before we lose our heads," Jillian said. "We need an accountant and we need to let Jake know that we have found the money. Technically, this belongs to them too and we need to do the right thing, Ian."

"Do you think dear Aunt Carla would have split the money with us if she would have found it? I seriously doubt it, Jillian," Ian replied sarcastically.

"Listen Ian, that doesn't matter, we need to do the right thing because we are people with morals. This money needs to be split up four ways."

Jillian asked Karen if she knew of an accountant who could help them appraise the trunk's contents. Karen recommended a friend of her mothers, George Irving, a CPA in Hill City. Giving him a call, Jillian was surprised when he said that he could come out within a half hour. She got an odd feeling that he had been sitting there waiting for her to call or something, but dismissed the thought as her own paranoia.

The boys loaded the trunk onto a freight dolly and with great effort hauled it into the kitchen. Jillian put up the closed sign and told Karen and Roxie to take the rest of the day off with pay and she would call them as soon as they knew anything. When Mr. Irving finally arrived they were nearly jumping out of their skins with anticipation. They lay the booty out in front of him.

"Holy mackerel," he kept saying. "Let's get busy and see what we have here."

Putting on his glasses, he then pulled out a calculator, saying, "This is going to be just a rough estimate, and you realize of course the market changes daily, so the price of the stocks is going to be based on today only."

After he punched in some numbers he said, "She spent a pretty penny on this gold. Unfortunately, she probably bought when prices would have been really high. The gold has actually depreciated in value, which is a shame," he said.

"Gold was about eight hundred an ounce in…when do you think she did this anyway?"

"As near as we can figure, 1978 or '79." Jillian added, "We don't know for sure."

"Well, in 1978 gold was at an all time high and it has never been as valuable since. I'm going to figure it at four hundred dollars per ounce. That's closer to today's gold prices."

Continuing to add the numbers he estimated, "The gold may bring 225 to 325 thousand dollars. Kids, what we are looking at here is… maybe eight million dollars. This railroad stock was the best thing she did, actually, because it has increased four fold since she bought it."

He stopped talking and looks at them.

"What are your plans?" he asked.

"Drink tequila, have a party?" Ian smiled then looked at his sister intently. "Sir, we are splitting all of this four ways with our two cousins, and we are going to set up a trust fund to take care of our aunt and uncle, who are injured."

Jillian gave her brother a robust hug. "I knew you would do the right thing. I knew because you are a decent and honest person, Ian Moore."

Chapter 22
The Present

Heath had been a busy little beaver when he had gone back to California. He was determined to give Jillian the deed for the campground as a wedding present and was having a law firm in Rapid City do some detective work, trying to check on the status of the property. No one was sure exactly who owned it.

From talking to Ian, Heath understood that back in 1979 some investors had purchased it through their grandmother but he needed to find out who they were and whether they would be willing to sell it to him.

Time was getting short, August was just around the corner and Heath was getting impatient. Finally, nearing the end of July, he got word from them.

"Mr. Connors, this is Larry Siegrist," the lawyer announced to Heath. "Sir, I finally found the owner of the campground and I don't think she really wanted to hear from me. She said no, the campground is definitely not for sale."

"Did you get a name? She may talk to me," Heath explained.

"I doubt it, but you can try. Her name is Roseanne Sanderson, and her address is listed in Hill City, so she's a local. From what I could ascertain she inherited it from her father in 1979. His name was Martin Moore."

"Did you say Roseanne Sanderson? She is the daughter of Martin Moore?"

"Yes sir, the original deed listed the buyer as Martin Investments, but it turned out only one guy actually owned it. They have both operated the business under an assumed identity."

Heath couldn't believe what he was hearing. "You're absolutely sure, Mr. Siegrist?"

"Absolutely, Mr. Connors, I'm positive."

Heath shuffled slowly over to the lodge, contemplating this unfortunate turn of events, which was not only going to stir up his bride-to-be but was also going to put a big crimp in his wedding gift plans.

He had imagined buying the campground and running it with Jillian at his side, just as her grandparents had done. Knowing she would never leave St. Elmo's Silverbell Lodge, he had made plans for his future around her. Restoring the resort to its original splendor, not fractured into separate entities, and raising his children here, beside the woman he loved, was his greatest expectation.

"It would be such a wholesome environment for them," he mumbled as he walked toward the kitchen. "Jillian works too hard, she needs some help around here. She needs pampered and I just happen to up for the job, but not this job, not breaking this news to her. She's had about enough excitement for one week already."

"What! What do you mean Martin Moore owned the campground?" she asked as she stood up from the table. The room begins to do that weird thing it always did when she stood up too fast.

"He's our grandfather, Heath, no way; he disappeared when my father was a boy. He died or something," she responded.

Jillian sat down and put her head in her arms as a fainting spell began to come over her.

Ian, totally dumbstruck, asked Jillian if she was okay.

"Yeah, I think I'm okay. This is just such a shock to me."

"That's only half of it, Jillian." Heath looked at Ian and then put his arm around Jillian's shoulder to help cushion the blow.

"His daughter is Roseanne Sanderson, Karen's mom!"

Heath leaned back in the chair, fully expecting Jillian to scream or pound the table or cry, but when she didn't, he continued on, "She inherited the campground in 1979, but she has other people run it for her so you wouldn't ever know she had any part in it."

"Oh, my god," Jillian sighed. "If Roseanne is Martin Moore's' child and my dad and Aunt Carla are his children too, they are half brothers and sisters. That means Karen is our cousin, Ian. This is just too crazy to possibly be true. Heath, are you sure about this?"

"Yes, Jillian, I had a lawyer check into it," he replied.

"Why did you do that?" Jillian was confused, finding that this made no sense to her whatsoever.

"I don't really want to tell you but under these circumstances I guess I had better let the cat out of the bag. I wanted to give the campground to you as a wedding present."

Standing up abruptly, Jillian left the table. Walking through the dining room and back to her apartment, she fell face first into the pillow on her bed and tried to make sense of what all had happened.

Realizing he had just laid an elephant in her lap, Heath followed her. Lying softly beside her he whispered quietly into her beautiful brunette hair, "Are you angry with me, Jillian?"

Rolling over, she wrapped herself around him and professed, "I could never be angry with you. I love you with all my heart. I can't believe you would do something like that for me. Heath, that campground is expensive; it's also a huge responsibility. It would take a pretty big effort on your part to run it because there is no way I can do that too."

"I thought that we could hire a couple to run the campground in the summers, and maybe get some more help at the lodge too. I just want you to be my queen and run your kingdom from your throne, not work your fingers to the bone. I have money too, Jillian, plenty of money. What I want most is for you to have time, time for yourself, time with me, time to spend with us as a family."

"That's what I want too, Heath, I want us to be a family," she replied. "How do you think your kids are feeling about this? It's going to be a huge adjustment for them, you know."

"I know, but I can tell they loved it here because they didn't want to leave. I told them they would be back when we get married, only this time for good. They are both excited about that. They think you're great. They saw how you are—kind and decent."

"Thank you, you're sweet, Heath, but it's still going to be an adjustment…for all of us. How did you find out all that information about the campground anyway?" she wondered.

He smiled. "I told you I was snoopy and I mean it. I just have a natural curiosity about things and ever since I first heard that story about your grandmother selling that campground out from under your aunt for less than its full price I've been suspicious. Then, one thought led to another and I decided that your family needed it back so I did the research. I'm so sorry it turned out the way it did."

"What's going on around here anyway? This is a terrible revelation to me, just mindboggling."

That evening the three musketeers congregated in front of a fire that Ian had made in the dining room. This day has had all of the excitement and drama they could handle. Ian and Heath decided to have a couple of beers and Jillian decided to join them.

"We have us a mystery here, now don't we?" Ian began. "We have a treasure chest full of money that Grandma supposedly buried about the same time Martin Moore showed up and bought the campground."

He continued, "Grandma sold that campground for one–fourth of its actual value. I think she knew who Martin Investments was, don't you?"

"Maybe old Marty came back and gave her a bad time about something," Heath added.

"Exactly how does Bert fit into this picture? Bert just shows up the next spring. I think if we pay close attention to the time table it will account for something here," Jillian added, waving her hand in the air.

"The only thing he accounts for, Jillian, is two murders. One of which I am a possible suspect in," Ian replied.

"I believe Roseanne Sanderson has some esplaining to do. I think we should pay her a visit tomorrow," Ian suggested in a Ricky Ricardo accent.

"I feel so betrayed by her, Ian. She moved here from Missouri, you know, she probably followed her evil, scheming father right to South Dakota. Maybe Karen doesn't know about this. She's been my best friend since I was sixteen." Jillian said, surprised by the slur in her speech already.

She was feeling the beer going straight to her head and thinking how good it felt to numb the intensity of her emotions right then. She thought about how horrible the accident had been for her aunt and uncle, yet a wonderful but unexpected marriage proposal soon followed for her.

Next, she thought about how they found the money on the Sleeping Abe while preparing for her wedding and then learned that Martin Moore had been across the street, probably watching her and Ian and they didn't even know it.

Lastly, she felt stung by a betrayal from someone she had known and trusted like a mother and as if that weren't enough, they were dealing with another possible murder on the Sleeping Abe. It was too much! Jillian opened another bottle of beer and slugged it down, feeling sorry for herself, sorry for her aunt and uncle, and angry at Roseanne Sanderson.

Jillian could tell she was getting drunk, but she didn't care right now.

Money, stupid money, she thought.

She hated money right now, loathing how it changed people. Jillian was certain that Martin Moore was after Grandma's money. Why else would he come and find her? Why else would she be hiding it? Grandma wanted everyone to think she didn't have any left and that Bert had spent it all.

Well death caught up with all of them anyway, but the sad part about it was they were still playing the game that started 25 years ago. *Maybe it was just a Jumanji game; maybe this wasn't real and if we finished the game everything will return to normal. Daddy would be alive, Mommy would still be here, Grandma and Grandpa would be happily running their little resort and I would be a little girl again.*

"Jillian, are you okay?" Heath asked her as her head bobbed limply around her shoulders.

"No. I think I'm drunk. Put me to bed. I don't think I can get there by myself," she said as she tried unsuccessfully to stand up and fell back into the chair.

"What a lightweight! You never could hold your alcohol," Ian chimed in. "Let's get you to bed, little sister."

"But she only had two beers, Ian; can you actually get drunk on two beers?" Heath asked.

"She can, obviously." Ian laughed as they got on either side of her and helped her back to the apartment. "Heath, get her undressed. It wouldn't be right if I did," he chuckled as he threw Heath a nightgown he had found in her top drawer.

Heath finally managed to wrestle her clothes off of her and get her dressed in night clothes.

"You're too good to me, Heath, I'm not used to it."

"Get used to it, Cookie." He kissed her softly on the forehead and covered her up.

"Hey, remind me not to encourage her to drink, okay?" he said to Ian as they walked back to the fireplace.

"She doesn't drink very often and she can't weigh much more than one hundred and twenty pounds. She's a lightweight and I love her for it," Ian said. They picked up their beer bottles and threw them in the trash.

"Heath, you should stay over here in case she gets sick. Sleep on the bunk bed if you want." Ian knew Heath wanted to wait until they were married to be with his sister. He doubted if he would ever be so noble with a woman.

Ian and Heath continue to visit into the night, long after Jillian goes to sleep.

"Where are you planning to live, Heath? There really isn't a suitable house on this property to live in and I think her apartment is neat but not suited for a family of four."

"I've been thinking about that, Ian. I had hoped to buy the campground so we could build a house in the meadow behind those rocks that look like stacked books. It's flat and has a view of the granite spires that is breathtaking, but now it seems as if the campground is out of the question. I'm stymied right now as to what we'll do."

Heath finished his beer. "But tomorrow is a new day. We'll see what providence throws at us tomorrow. I'm going to bed. Goodnight, Ian."

"Goodnight," Ian said as he headed over to the old house to sleep.

Chapter 23
Greed Comes Calling

Heath found that he was having trouble falling asleep with Jillian so near. He felt as if he was in a twilight sleep, aware of her breathing and her movements in the night. Still being semi-awake, he heard the door creak out in the dining room, which instantly bought him to full consciousness. Was someone breaking in or did Ian forget something over here?

Just then he watched a flashlight beam tracking its way across the floor in the dining room and it became apparent to him that someone was breaking into the lodge.

Damn, we didn't lock the front door, too much beer makes a man careless, he thought.

The trunk was hidden in Jillian's closet, covered loosely with a blanket. He quickly realized that he and Ian had put Jillian in danger without even thinking about it.

It's a darned good thing I decided to stay, he said to himself as he quietly pulled back the covers and prepared to take action against the intruders.

On hands and knees he crawled silently across the room where he hid behind the French doors leading out to the dining room and waited. Jillian had put heavy sheers up on the doors for privacy, yet he could still see the flashlight through them.

Whoever it was was coming his way. Heath could hear two voices, trying to be as quiet as they could on the creaking wooden floor yet being stupid enough to whisper to each other. Feeling around for something to hit them with if he needed to, his fingers connected with his boot strings—the steel-toed work boots he had worn to move the rock earlier in the day.

Quietly the French door opened a little at a time. Unfortunately for them, the first one through the door gets the full brunt of the steel-toe right in their face. Swinging as hard as he could, Heath successfully knocked them both to the ground in one swift movement, creating a domino effect of falling bodies.

Groping around in the darkness, Heath finally connected with the light switch, standing to the side just in case they had a gun. Startled awake by the commotion, Jillian sat up and screamed, which gives Heath an opportunity to jump on top of the one that was still moving.

"Jillian, call the police," he ordered.

Deputy Sheriff Glen Randall got to the lodge quickly—very quickly. Heath thought that he had spotted him "in the area" quite a bit lately and suspected he has been keeping an eye on the place since the accident. Heath was grateful for that at the moment.

"I thought I would be hearing from you again," he said as he came through the door of the dining room. "What's going on here?"

After listening to Heath's version of the break-in, Officer Randall cuffed the perpetrators and sat each of them on a dining room chair, securing their feet to a table leg. Bleeding profusely from his nose was the little man that Heath had come to know as Jon Harden, Karen's supposed boyfriend.

Ian came bounding through the door. Jillian had called him in a panic, saying there were robbers in the lodge. He was relieved the police were already there.

Jillian, realizing that the burglar was none other than Roseanne Sanderson, thought it would be best to let Ian and Heath take care of it. She just couldn't face this woman right now; this liar who had pretended to care about her but was just using her to get what she wanted.

Roseanne was read her Miranda Rights. She was asked if she understood that anything she said could be used against her in a court of law. She vehemently hissed that she understood but began to talk anyway. A virtual floodgate of emotion begins to flow from her mouth as thirty years of keeping up a charade of secrecy and deceit has taken a toll on her.

Roseanne screamed at Ian, barring her teeth like a rabid animal.

"Half of the money you found belongs to me! My father was Martin Moore. He didn't divorce your Grandma Lugenia. She didn't have any legal right marrying that Crawford guy because she was still legally married to my father. That means half of her money belonged to my father. If it belonged to my father, then it now belongs to me."

"So, Martin Moore is a part of all this? You mean the dear old school teacher who abandoned his wife and two kids? Nice guy, your father, a real peach. What did he do, blackmail my grandmother?"

"My dad wanted to have some leverage on her is all. She was an evil person, keeping what was rightfully his all to herself," she sobbed as black mascara ran down the deep wrinkles in her face.

"Don't you mean Grandpa dear extorted the campground so that he could keep an eye on us and possibly use Jillian and I as a bargaining chip? Maybe he even threatened to kill us if she didn't pay him what he was asking?" Ian retorted.

"My father would never hurt you. He was an old man. He just wanted what was due him. That's all."

"Yeah right, Roseanne. Grandma practically gave him that campground and I know darned good and well she wouldn't have unless he was threatening her or her family. She gave him the campground but apparently that wasn't enough for him. "

"Why should we settle for the campground when she had all of our money too? Daddy deserved his share of her money."

"How about you, how did you get involved in this?" Ian continued to press her, knowing full well the police officer was taping the whole thing.

"My father told me all about his plans. I am his favorite child, he loved me the best. He didn't marry my mother but he loved her more than he loved your grandmother."

Ian snickered at how insanely childish she sounded.

"Daddy always thought Bert was just a ploy," she continued. "He was a decoy to convince us she was spending all her millions on him. We suspected Lugenia had hid the rest of the money somewhere on the Sleeping Abe because Daddy saw her bringing the front-end loader down from there one day for no apparent reason. It was suspicious looking, because she was never known to drive any of the heavy equipment around. Not since I first moved here had I ever seen that woman drive a tractor. She was up to something and we both knew it.

"Later on, Daddy hid behind the trees and watched that stupid Bert digging holes up there. He knew what Bert was doing; he was looking for the same thing we wanted—the money. But you see I'm the one who actually told Bert there might be money buried up on the Sleeping Abe in the first place. He was looking for the money because I had accidentally told him it was there."

"What? How did you get mixed up with Bert?" Ian asked, still unsure of the connection.

"One night I got a little drunk at the bar in town. I didn't know who Bert was. He was buying me drinks, and I just told him too much that night. He tricked me into telling him what Daddy and I were doing. I told him who we were; that we had been watching Lugenia Crawford because we thought she had some money that she was trying to keep from us. That was when Bert decided to start courting her, and started looking for the money himself. I think that Bert expected my father to show up on the Sleeping Abe sooner or later," she sniffed.

"Did your father confront Bert?" Ian asks.

"Yes, Daddy had to stop him from finding the money so he went up to the Sleeping Abe with a gun. Daddy was going to kill him but Bert was ready for him. They fought over the gun but Bert was so much younger than Daddy that he overpowered him and hit him in the head with a shovel instead. I went up there trying to stop my father but I was too late. He was already dead."

"Martin Moore died when Bert hit him in the head with the

shovel?" Ian asked, totally dumbstruck. "Well at least I'm off the hook."

"I must remind you, Ms. Sanderson, that you have been read you're Miranda Rights and that what you say can be used against you; now you do understand that, right?"

"Yes, I understand what you're saying, but I need to let Ian know why half of that money is mine," she insisted and kept right on talking.

Becoming more hysterical, she continued, "Bert threatened me; he said he would go to the police and tell them I was involved in a blackmailing scheme if I didn't help him take care of Daddy's body. I didn't want to go to jail so I did whatever Bert wanted. He made me help him, I didn't want too."

"I have an idea how you helped Bert. You helped conceal the body, didn't you?"

"Bert and I threw him into the old elevator shaft up on the Sleeping Abe. Bert pulled that big pulley system down on top of him so no one could climb into that shaft and find him."

"Yeah, and how did that work for you?" Ian pushed her on, still trying to get the whole story out of her.

Fighting frantically against the tie on the chair she yelled at Officer Randall, "You let me go! They are the thieves; they're stealing money that belongs to me."

She spit manically towards Ian, "Your grandmother broke the law too, you know—it's called bigamy. Half of her money belonged to my dad because she was still married to him. Damn you, don't you get it?"

"Oh, I think he gets it, lady, seems to me you're the one who doesn't get it," Officer Randall remarked. "We're going to be taking a little ride into Rapid City and get you some help."

Jillian swung the French doors open and walked straight up to Roseanne.

"Does Karen know about this?" she hissed vehemently in Roseanne's face. Tears were the last emotion Jillian wanted Roseanne to see in her. She wants her to see hate, though after hearing Roseanne's confession she felt deep pity for her. Jillian realized that Roseanne was another victim of greed.

"No, your highness, my daughter knows nothing. We kept her in the dark, she's innocent," replied Roseanne.

"What about Jillian? Ian asked. "Didn't you care what happened to her?"

"Are you kidding?" Roseanne laughed deviously. "When Karen and Jillian met I knew it was Providence. I befriended Jillian so I would know if you two ever found that money and finally you did. It was easy."

Ian realized Roseanne Moore Sanderson was insane, just like Aunt Carla had become insane, over money. Not even money, for they had never had it in their possession, but just the possibility of it was enough to drive them over the edge. Roseanne had concealed a murder, had illegally disposed of a body, was an accessory to blackmail, and now she would be charged for breaking and entering.

Jillian posed the question, "Who killed my grandmother?"

"Ha, that was a no-brainer! My dad knew all about your grandma, after all he was married to her. She loved chocolate. Daddy shot the mercury and cyanide into chocolate candy bars with a needle and mailed them to her right before his accident. He wrote her a note saying it was from some group in the hills that wanted to thank her for having the best business of the month. She bought it hook, line and sinker. To bad he died before she did though, he wanted to watch her. He thought she deserved it."

Jillian reared back and slapped Roseanne across the face. Quickly, Ian grabbed Jillian and held her as she yelled, "You heartless bitch!"

"Why did he want to kill her?" Ian asked as Officer Randall, realizing the situation had become too explosive, began to lead Roseanne toward the door.

Roseanne was certain that she was going to have the last possible word. "You know, it's kind of funny how both Bert and Lugenia used each other as a means to an end. She was going to go to the police; she had hid the money nice and secure and she knew if she could convince a judge she had spent it all on Bert, it didn't matter if she was married or not. She may have out-schemed my dad, but not me, because you two are going to pay for the mistakes of your precious grandmother."

"Ian, are you finished talking to her?" Officer Randall asked.

"Just one more thing sir. How is it that Karen's boyfriend Jon is here if Karen doesn't know anything about this?"

"She paid me and that's all I have to say without a lawyer."

Officer Randall loaded Roseanne Sanderson and Jon Harden into the police vehicle.

"I'm going to need all three of you to come in and write out statements for me," he said. "I want to see you in the station tomorrow before noon."

He gave them the address of the station and his cell phone number in case anything else came up and quietly left St Elmo's Silver Bell Lodge, no sirens this time.

They've had enough trouble, he thought as he headed down the winding road.

Chapter 24
And In Conclusion

The very next day Jillian made the decision to close the restaurant for the rest of the season. It was just getting to be too much of a burden, considering the extent of the problems they had dealt with the last two weeks.

She felt exhausted. The stress has caused her to lose weight and her skin looked sallow and old. She needed some time—time to recover from this travesty of greed and time to get to know her potential husband better before she jumped into something she might possibly regret for the rest of her life.

Dutifully she went to the police station and filed a report, along with Ian and Heath. Her heart was aching from the loss of someone she considered to be a friend, aching from the betrayal of family against family.

Ian divided the money up between the four cousins fairly and equitably. He put one million dollars in a trust fund to pay for Victor and Carla's medical bills and their rent in a well respected assisted living center in California. Uncle Victor had been flown back to California on the very day the trunk was discovered.

They each received one-and-a-half million dollars. Ian donated one hundred thousand dollars to the rescue services involved in the recovery of his aunt and uncle, and the same amount to the Pennington County Police Department for always being there when they were needed. He wrote a check to his newfound half-cousin Karen for five hundred thousand dollars, and invested the remaining three hundred thousand in the bank to help fund a new project he was hoping to start.

Ian couldn't help but be amazed at the amount of misery this money had caused. He vowed he would do everything in his power to help the underprivileged with his share of it.

He confided in Jillian that he wanted to build a camp on the Sleeping Abe for children from needy families and he wondered if she would be interested in pooling their finances. They could turn the lodge into the dining hall for the campers, and build cabins for sleeping.

Of course, they were going to need horses for trail rides and a barn to keep them in. He would dam the streambed and create a lake above the old mill to canoe in, and of course they could catch fish in the pond at the lodge.

They would let their little campers pan for gold in the shaker box and teach them the importance of caring for the environment. They both agreed this camp would be based on Christian values, something neither of them knew much about but with Heath's encouragement were willing to find out.

Jillian took exactly two seconds to decide that this was a fantastic idea. She would be surrounded with children, blessed beyond her wildest imagination. Heath knew that this was his future as well, as he has always wanted to minister to people, and this would be exactly the environment he had been looking for his own children. Together they sat and designed the camp: where the cabins would be located, the barn, the bathrooms, the shower facilities, and the housing for the staff.

They considered their staff and decided that a group of college–aged young adults would work best to feed the spiritual needs of their campers. They would look for people who were musical, upbeat and positive.

They would need cooks, lifeguards and counselors, but most of all they would need each other to support and trust each other when the tough decisions needed to be made.

They knew that they must never squabble over the money. Taking an oath, they declared their loyalty to the project and to each other, needing no advice on the dangers of becoming greedy. That lesson had been forever embedded in their souls and was, in effect, their true inheritance. They drank a toast of club soda to seal the contract.

In August, Heath and Jillian wed on the Sleeping Abe and Heath moved his little family into the old house while a two-story addition was built off of Jillian's apartment at the lodge.

Karen had taken over the operation of the campground and Heath and Jillian tried to help her as often as they could, welcoming her into the family with open arms. Ian began to date Roxie, Jillian's waitress, and they were fast becoming a committed couple.

The camp opened its doors in the spring of 2005, starting a new and better chapter for the descendants of Martin Moore and Lugenia Crawford. The emphasis here was on love, goodness and charity, not deceit and deception. Heath and Jillian begin their new life together, wrapped in the arms of unending possibilities and of course, each other.

Roseanne Sanderson's lawyer pleaded an insanity defense for her and won, causing her to be hospitalized for one year and then released under the supervised care of a psychiatrist. She came to Jillian and Ian and apologized for the trouble she had caused, begging for their forgiveness.

Jillian suggested to her that she become a cook for the children's camp and tearfully she agreed. Jillian followed the old adage, *"Keep your friends close but your enemies closer"* with Roseanne. Though she had forgiven her, she would never again trust her.

Roseanne was certain she had convinced Jillian and everyone else that she was rehabilitated. "Now that I'm on the inside, getting my money should be a piece of cake," she declared as she licked frosting off of her finger. "Yes sir, a piece of cake!"

Author Biography

Married to her sweetheart, Bill, Jill Kreutzer is the mother of two daughters, Kayla and Deena, and a son, Evan. *The Pinkest Rose* was written while they were living in Edgemont, South Dakota, Jill's hometown, and was truly a family effort.

Jill's grandparents were uranium miners in the Edgemont area in the 1950s and most of the geographical information is true. The story is entirely fabricated, though Jill's grandmother did actually lie down in front of a bulldozer to stop claim jumpers from mining their claims, and they did own and operate St. Elmo's Silver Belle Lodge and Campground in the 1950s and '60s.

Jill's parent's still live in South Dakota and her father and stepmother live in the old house mentioned in the story.

Now living in Amarillo, Texas, Bill is working for the BNSF Railroad and Jill is currently working as a quality assurance associate for a major distribution center. They plan to retire where the taxes are low, the weather is warm, or in close proximity to their future grandchildren.

Printed in the United States
50738LVS00002B/127-135